Penguin Book 2434

Sleep-Walkers

David Karp was born in New York City in 1922
and lived there until 1942, when he enlisted
in the United States Army and served in the
Philippines and in Japan.

On leaving the Army in 1946 he continued
his interrupted education, and graduated from
the College of the City of New York in 1948. After
college he became a continuity writer for a
New York radio station, and he has since done
intensive work in this field and in television. He
won a Guggenheim fellowship for fiction in
1956. His first book, *One,* which he published
in 1954, was a great critical and popular success
and was followed by *The Day of the Monkey*
(1955), *All Honourable Men* (1956), *Leave Me Alone*
(1958), and *The Last Believers* (1964). His short
stories have appeared in many magazines.
David Karp was married in 1944 and has two
sons.

Sleep-Walkers

David Karp

Penguin Books

Penguin Books Ltd, Harmondsworth,
Middlesex, England
Penguin Books Pty Ltd, Ringwood,
Victoria, Australia

First published in the U.S.A. as *Enter, Sleeping* 1960
Published in Great Britain by Victor Gollancz 1960
Published in Penguin Books 1966
Copyright © David Karp, 1960

Made and printed in Great Britain by
C. Nicholls & Company Ltd
Set in Linotype Pilgrim

Dedicated with love to Ethan
and to Andrew and, most of
all, to Lillian.

He kissed her and put his hand under her sweater to find her breast. Although small and warm, it was satisfyingly firm.

'You must meet my family,' she murmured into his cheek.

'Yes, yes,' he replied with all the agreeableness of a young man whose attentions are elsewhere. Then, with a deftness he had not thought her capable of, he was inside the house and her father was staring at him. Although he was not certain he was her father. And yet the squareness of the face was there, the blondness of the hair, the faded blue of the eyes, the solid, silent manner. The quickness and the bluntness. The regularity of Teutonic stupidity was there. And yet not stupidity. Not even dullness. Not even blandness. What? Suppressed anger. Why suppressed? Out of fear? Not fear. Out of shame? Out of a sense of propriety?

'This is Julius,' she said to the man.

'I guessed as much,' her father said. And the voice was like her voice and yet a man's voice. Flat, quick, literal. It said what it said. No more, no less. It was like her. 'Sit down,' her father said. 'Be comfortable here.'

He sat and waited. She walked out of the room, without an explanation, without a promise, without a word. That was like her. It disconcerted him but his hand still remembered the shape of her breast and he was willing to forgo much to renew the memory.

'What do you do?' her father asked as he sat opposite

him. His manner, his posture were the same. Flat, calm, unassailable, impenetrable.

'I work for a stage producer,' he said.

'But what do you do?' he was asked again.

'I read plays.'

'Towards what end?'

'To inform the producer which plays are good.'

'Does he take your advice?'

'He reads what I recommend he read.'

'And does he produce what you recommend he produce?'

'Not very often.'

The man paused for a moment. 'Do you find that satisfying?'

He considered the question for a moment, and something flickered through her father's blue eyes. What was it? Pleasure? 'I haven't thought of it that way.'

'Then why do you do it at all?'

'Because I need a job. I have to eat, to live.'

'You don't have to live,' her father said with a voice that was almost kindly. 'If you find life burdensome, I know a doctor who will provide you with a poison which is almost painless.'

He sat up straight in his chair alarmed. 'That's not what I meant. I mean – I want to live.'

'Towards what end?' her father asked, his voice still free of malice or sneers. The voice had one quality, an implacable curiosity.

'I want to write songs,' he said.

'And do you write songs?'

'Yes, whenever I can.'

'Do they satisfy you?'

'Yes, yes, they do. Only I wish –' he paused, uncertain. How did he go on?

'Yes, you wish what?'

'I wish others would like them enough to publish them.'

'Then they do not satisfy you?' the man pressed and yet did not press. Rather, he moved forward.

'They're good songs. They're great songs.'

'But other people don't think so.'

'Not everyone thinks so,' he corrected the older man. and almost, but not quite, thought to himself, You have a nerve!

'And you won't be happy with your songs until everyone thinks they are as good as you think they are?'

'Well, to be honest – yes.'

Her father looked at him with a sudden look of surprise. 'Why did you say that?'

'Why did I say what?'

'To be honest – haven't you been honest?'

'Of course I have!' he said a little sharply, and wanted to add, 'you damned fool.' But did not. He was her father.

'Something can be good without meeting the standards of other people,' he said, and the younger man was confused. Was he finished with his honesty? That was accepted, was it? Now what had he said? Oh, yes, to be sure.

'I know it can,' he said. 'My stuff is good.'

The girl came out with a tray with three thick mugs on it. The steam curled from them. 'Do you like cocoa?' she asked.

'Yes, of course,' he replied, grateful that she had come in. She handed a mug to her father first and then one to him and took one for herself. She sat down on the sofa and tucked her legs under her. Her legs, he noticed again as being particularly good. Slim and yet shapely. Sitting in the same frame of reference as her father, he could see the strong family resemblance. A hell of a father-in-law he would make! Luckily, not for him. He had a tigerish impulse but erased it from his mind and tried to look the kitten. The harmless kitten. He licked the cocoa and smiled at her. She did not smile back. She looked at him forthrightly over her cup. The same faded blue eyes. He could look from hers to her father's. Tick, tock. Blue, blue. Same shade. Same intensity.

'And what do you think of my father?' she asked.

His intestines, caught by surprise, froze against one another while the interior system of alarms flickered and jangled and tried to single out the source of attack. The internal result was disaster, and the brain defected to the autonomic nervous system. He hiccoughed in defence. If he had been a lower order of mammal, he would have urinated in confused reprisal.

'Your father,' he said, and hiccoughed again, 'is an honest man.'

She turned to her father. 'And what do you think of Julius?'

'He is a fool,' her father said calmly.

'I beg your pardon,' he said, too surprised to hiccough.

'Why?' her father asked.

'Why?!' he asked, angry.

'Why do you beg his pardon?' she asked.

He looked at both of them, father and daughter. The same puzzled look in their faces. Ah, the family resemblance goes deeper than the pigmentation of the eyes, the shape of the bones. It goes past the skull into the brain. They are the same. Nuts. Nut, nut. Tick, tock. 'I resent being called a fool,' he said, not too fervently. The shape still remembered in the hand could be inspected by eye. Through a sweater, of course. But still there. Still warm, no doubt. And still firm, to be sure. Still small and round, on inspection.

'That's reasonable,' her father said. She nodded faintly, as if she agreed.

He looked at both of them, angry. They were not nuts. They were jokers. A pair of jokers. Very well, joke away. His would be the last laugh. When he had her, and he would have her, he'd take her wearing dirty socks. Let them laugh that off. 'I don't expect to be called a fool when I haven't done or said anything foolish,' he replied. The important thing was to preserve an air of earnestness. Let them think him earnest. Solemn, even. She'd find out what kind of a fool he was. Ha, ha, *ha!*

'I am bored with you,' her father said, rising from his chair and putting down the cocoa mug. 'Aren't you bored with him yet?'

'I've only just met him this afternoon,' she said to her father. 'He was most helpful in the rain.'

'He is incapable of being helpful,' her father replied. 'He's witless, helpless, sightless. He is like all the other sleep-walkers.'

He retreated behind his cocoa cup as he listened. Jokers, jokers. He hummed, to himself, a scrap of melody which he had been chasing all day. Sleep-walkers. Not a bad title. How would it go into the lyric? *I'm sleep-walking over you. I toss and turn the whole night through ... I'm helpless ... breathless ... sleepless over you ... over you ... babee ... I'm just helpless, helpless, helpless over youuuu....*

She patted the place on the couch beside her, and he came out of his creative reverie to see that her father was gone. He put down the cup and almost skipped to the couch and plumped himself down beside her. 'I guess I didn't make a hit with your dad,' he said.

'No,' she said softly, without regret, and put an exploratory finger in his hair. 'You are not wearing a hair piece?'

'I should say not!' he said vigorously. 'What do you take me for? I'm only twenty-four!' He pulled at his hair. 'Real, real, every strand of it!'

She laughed softly, and it changed the shape of her face, the colour of her eyes. 'Sing me one of your songs.'

'Your father just gave me an idea for one. Do you have a piano around here?' He looked about the room. She pulled at the lobe of his ear.

'I said sing – not play.'

He placed his muzzle against her cheek. 'Which one do you want to hear?' His hand moved cautiously but she anticipated him and grasped his wrist and pushed his hand under her sweater. His tiny network of glands sprang into action, putting sweat in his armpits, putting his legs to sleep, and arousing his loins. Hey, hey! His lips rubbered along her neck and found her ear. He looked through the golden filaments of her hair and saw the door to the next room. Her father! He moved away.

'Don't you think we ought to go some place more private?' he asked.

'Why?' she asked.

'Oh, I may find myself uncontrollable,' he said gaily, worrying that the word was too strong.

'But who wants to control you?' she asked mildly.

'I may want to control myself. I *do* want to control myself.'

'In that case,' she said, moving away from him, 'you will also bore me.'

He looked at her, surprised, alarmed, frightened. What's this? He waited, shrinking back a little, shrinking inside of his skin. He was no fool. Not born yesterday, by God. What was he doing here? Sure he had an umbrella and sure he let her share it three blocks to the subway and he had an extra token and rode with her and bought her newspaper and gave her at least half of what she needed to buy a bag of rolls. But what of it? What did that make him? Looking at it coldly, and that was the only way to look at things – coldly – what had he done to get all he was getting? At the door he had stopped to make a date, say good-bye. And she moved against him. Well, all right, it had happened before. It wasn't implausible. And getting his hand under her sweater. Well, that was a lot. That was the cherry on top of the whipped cream, so to speak. To be taken in and introduced to the family. That had happened before. Oh, God, how many times. But to be treated by her father like that. That had not happened before. Not while he was awake, at least. It had happened in his dreams. In his dreams he had stopped before people who had looked at him and shook their heads in pity and smiled and he had grabbed himself to look. What was wrong with him? Did his breath stink? Was he fat or bald? Were his shoes unshined, his hair greasy, his socks the wrong colour? Was his suit too cheap, his tie too flashy, his education deficient? Was his penis too small, his nose too large, his teeth too ragged, his smile unfriendly, his armpits rich, his vocabulary betraying him? Did his false teeth slip, his truss show, his grey hair tell his age? Was his blood, nerves, brain or feet tired? And yet they laughed and snickered and pitied and smiled, and he had awakened tense, breathless, sweating, anxious. God, there were so many things to guard against! But this was not a dream. This was reality. This sofa, that girl, that chair, that cocoa cup, that man, those words. All real. And in the real world no one ever said 'I am bored with you.' In the real world no neat, soft, curved, golden bundle such as this snuggled up to him within an hour and a half, dragged him on a couch fifteen minutes later, talked cold turkey in twenty minutes, and after ten seconds of casual necking suggested he wasn't fast enough. What

was she? A nymphomaniac? A schizoid? A manic de-
pressive? A female satyr? Or was it something colder,
cooler. Cool, man cool. Was that her father? In a pig's
eye, it was. He smiled at her now. So that was the old
dodge, heh? She cruised in the rain to find a likely sucker,
dragged him up to the 'house', introduced him to her
'father', exchanged a few pleasantries, slipped a little
Spanish fly into the cocoa, 'father' withdrew, daughter
heated up the sucker, and when he was about to com-
mit the ramming home, in popped poppa waving her
birth certificate. She is less than eighteen. Here it is.
Plain print. I call the cops and get fifteen, twenty years
in prison. Help, help. No, no, don't call the police. I'll do
anything, anything. Pay us. Pay for what you have done
to this infant. Corrupting the morals of a minor is no
laughing matter in the sovereign state of New York. How
much is it worth to you? He checked himself. He had
one hundred and fifty-four dollars and sixty-six cents in
the Bowery Savings Bank, thirty-two dollars in his wallet, twelve dollars in nickels, dimes and quarters in a
small metal bank in the back of his dresser drawer, and
that was it. If they reduced him to his component elements, they couldn't get much more. Was it worth it?
Why would she pick him up in the street instead of in
some swanky bar? Couldn't they tell how much money
he didn't have? He eyed her. She looked more than eighteen. She was twenty-four if she was a day. Then what?
What, what, what, what? He smiled at her. Now he
knew. And *how* he knew! Same treatment. Same idea.
She picks up a handsome rugged young fellow. Doesn't
matter how much money he's got. They don't want him
for money. Oh, no, not *his* money. He just has to be big
and rugged and well-hung, and he had to admit that
he was all that. Gets him into the house, introduces the
fake 'father', a cup of cocoa with a dash of aphrodisiac

in his cup and *hers*. Then the poppa retreats. Retreats, all right, to a convenient observation spot behind six hundred dollars' worth of one-eyed machinery, gleaming, glistening, the sinister symbol *Leitz G.m.b.H.* engraved into the carefully machined surfaces. Stills, motion pictures. He had seen them himself, at lodges, at frat houses, in Legion halls, in meeting rooms, cellars, apartments, stags, smokers, bachelors' nights. Arts of Greece, Italy, Lesbos, Homos, the Neapolitan gambit. Ha, ha, that's it, all right.

Fumbling now with his lips, his hands, his eyelashes, her drawers, her lips, her hands, her eyelashes. 'Not here, Julius,' she said.

But, of course not here. Where's the set? Where are the lights?

The bedroom, of course – where else? She undresses herself swiftly, like a boxer stripping for the main event. And she undresses him, too. What's the hurry? Poppa running out of film? Why no lights? Infra-red photography?

He nuzzles against her cool flesh and peeks. Where's the lens? He doesn't want to show his face. Think how embarrassing it might be one day. First the standard stuff. He sighs and groans and murmurs into her ear. 'Where's the lens?'

She is tender and persuasive and yielding and guiding. He feels his bones bending with sweet agony. Oh, how perfect, how right D. H. Lawrence was! And Hemingway, you are right! he thought. The earth moves! It moves *Eppur si muove!* Where is the lens? He feels a great rush of tension; he is being raised upward, upward, upward in a giant fist for the final, terrible moment of intense compression and then the plummeting downward. He thinks as he is held aloft in the giant, mindless, boneless fist, with pride, with excitement, with joy, Look at me! Me, Julius Schapiro – a motion-picture star!

Act Two; Scene Three: Time, the next morning. Setting, the same. At curtain rise, the young lovers walk on. Roy sits down on the rocking chair on the porch. He turns his pale, exhausted young face towards the sun. Lulu Belle sits down on the porch steps looking up at him. There is adoration in her eyes. She adores Roy and she is frightened of losing him. When she speaks she is not speaking what she feels She is trying, desperately, to keep Roy with her.

LULU BELLE: Oh, God, it's going to be another scorcher, Roy. Can't you just feel it? I mean – I feel it here [*She touches her forehead*]
back of my eyes like. Whenever it's going to be like that I feel it back there. Ever since I was just a little 'un I could tell. Poppa used to say I was goin' to be a divinin' woman one day. I never truly met a divinin' woman. Did you, Roy, hunh Roy?

ROY: 'Scuse me, Lulu Belle.

LULU BELLE: Ever meet a divinin' woman I mean? Did you, Roy, did you?

ROY: I don't believe in that sort of thing.

LULU BELLE [*Getting up and swinging dreamily from the porch post*]: Oh, God, I do. Oh, yes, I do, I do. I believe in 'em. I believe in the future laying out there [*She extends a hand to the mysterious horizon*] all writ down and told out to the very last detail! And some folks, Roy – Roy?

ROY: I don't believe in it.

LULU BELLE: Oh, sure you do, Roy – sure you do! [*She rushes up the steps and almost into his lap but stops abruptly and just barely touches his shoulder with a delicate caressing motion*] Oh, God, Roy, you do have such clean-looking skin.

ROY: My God, Lulu Belle, you do jump about.

Julius took another bite of the soggy salami sandwich his mother had made for him, and flipped forward into the play.

MAMIE [*As she touches Roy's shoulders*]: Oh, Roy, you do have the sweetest body a boy ever did have. I could just touch you and touch you and touch you –

ROY: And what's Lulu Belle goin' to think if she finds us like this?

MAMIE: What the hell do I care what she thinks?

ROY: Well, you're a mother-woman, by God, and she's your daughter and I never saw a mother-woman carry on as you do and not carin' what her daughter thinks.

MAMIE: Roy – I'm a woman and there's been no man here in.

Julius took another sip of his Doctor Brown's Celery Tonic and flipped forward to the end of Act Two.

[*Lulu Belle rushes on stage. She looks about, bewildered.*]

LULU BELLE [*Softly at first*]: Roy? Roy? Roy, where are you? Roy? [*Her voice rises*] Roy, that's not fair hiding like that. I don't want to play that stupid ole game any more. Roy, do you hear me? [*Rushes about looking for him*] Roy, do you hear me? You come out right now! You come out right now, Roy, do you hear me? Do you hear? [*She puts her hand distractedly through her hair and collapses on the stage*] Roy, I don't want to play this stupid game any more. No, I give up. You win, Roy! You win, Roy! Roy! Roy! [*The curtain falls for the end of Act Two*]

Julius tossed the play aside and polished off his sandwich. 'Evelyn?' he said.

Evelyn looked up from her typing. 'When you're finished, you can take the mail out.'

'I'm stuck for a rhyme on "sleep-walker". What's another word for it?'

'Somnambulist,' she said, stripping an envelope from the carriage of the machine. Julius watched her tongue quickly lick the envelope. She made a face. 'We've either got to stop buying cheap stationery or get a rubber sponge. After about forty of these my mouth feels like the Chinese Army had done a march through it – with horses.'

'That's not much help – somnambulist,' Julius said thoughtfully. 'That's even tougher to fit into a rhyme scheme.'

'Why are you struggling, Julius? Why don't you give it up?'

'Because I've got some great lines for it – it's just sleep-walker that's got me stumped.'

'I don't mean the song. I mean song writing,' she said as she cranked another envelope up into her machine. 'It's a chump's way of earning a living. Do you think any decent girl will marry you if she finds out you want to be a song writer?'

'I'm not ready to get married,' Julius said nervously.

'Why are you fooling yourself?' She looked at him through thick, harlequin glasses. 'You were born a married man. There are some men born to be married just as there are some men born to fail in business. Like my brother-in-law. My parents keep pouring money into business after business. First it was a children's-wear store. Six months. Then it was a ladies'-dress shop. A year. Then he went into the storm-window business. Kaput in eleven months. Then partners in a bowling alley. Out in a year. A gas station, he falls on a patch of grease and ruptures himself, just in time, I might add. Another month and even the rupture wouldn't have saved him. One business after another, for twelve years, and the poor schnook can't make it. It's not that he doesn't work hard. He works and works and works. But he's unlucky, mismatched. He was born under the sign of bankruptcy with the mark of insolvency on his head. I'll bet he was wrapped in a summons when he was delivered. What are we going to do? Jerry is the baby sister. He's her husband. We keep it up. Why we keep it up I don't know. To make Jerry happy. For Christ's sakes, what the son of a bitch has cost us to keep Jerry happy we could have bought her a solid platinum priapus with a bagful of baguette emeralds.' She ripped out the envelope, inserted the letter, and ran her tongue wearily over the flap. 'Julius, you're a nice kid but you're living in the wrong world. Why don't you start looking up civil-service exams?'

'What? And bury myself in some poky little government job?'

'And what, may I ask, is so goddamned exalted about your present position?'

'I'm in show business,' he said with an injured air.

Evelyn snorted as he carefully balled up the waxed paper and dropped it into a can. He finished off the end of the celery tonic and then got up, discarded the straws, and went to the small sink to wash out the bottle. An old habit. He was compulsively clean. He'd get the three cents deposit without washing it out, but some racial memory took him to the sink. His mother still washed out milk bottles for the milkman. Who would think of leaving dirty milk bottles? Only swine and Irish slatterns would do something like that.

'I'm helpless, helpless, helpless without you, babee –' he sang at the sink, and peeked over his shoulder at Evelyn. 'Helpless, breathless, sleepless –'

'Oh, Jesus,' Evelyn said as she shook her head.

'Why, why Jesus!' he said, advancing on her with the dripping soda bottle. 'Go on, tell me what's wrong with that melody!'

She turned her broad, full face with her thick glasses up at him. 'There's nothing wrong with it, Julius. It's just as sticky-icky as all the *dreck* they write. Where do you think you're going to get if you're just like all the rest of them?'

'I've got talent,' he said stubbornly.

'For what?!' she snapped back.

'You said you liked some of my songs,' he said, retreating to little-boy defencelessness. That's what always got under Evelyn's corset. The little boy. Evelyn was a sucker for a little boy.

'I always like to say something nice about people,' she said, inserting another envelope. 'When you first came here you were made of soft caramels. Your face had no shape, your brains were held together with paper clips, and your soul looked like the beginning of a wart. Well, what can you say to such a thing? The Army didn't want you and your mother was ashamed to keep you at home any longer. You had to go some place and so you came here. That was five years ago, Julius. Five years ago! I said to myself: "To this thing I will be kind. Who knows what will happen if I am not kind? Perhaps it will fall apart and I will have to bring the slop home in a pail to your mother and then what would I say? Mrs Schapiro

– I was unkind to your puppy and he peed himself into this puddle? So I was kind. But to be kind one must be kind for something! What could I honestly say and be kind? The only thing I could find to be kind about were your terrible, awful songs. So I said a kind word about them. That was five years ago, Julius! Think! Think! Have I said a kind word about them since?'

He stared and looked at Evelyn, with her solid, round barrel body with its iron corset and its great strangled breasts and round unlined columnar throat, and wondered when last she had had a kind word to say about his songs. He could not remember. It seemed to him that lately, quite recently, she had said something complimentary but now he could not recall what and when. An odd feeling of unhappiness began to fill his face and he realized with horror that he might cry. He turned away and faced his employer, Mr Pollack.

'Good afternoon, good afternoon,' Mr Pollack said as he took off his coat with the ratty astrakhan collar and hung it up with his grease-spotted black fedora. He placed his yellowed cane against the wall. 'And how is the staff of Pollack Productions engaging itself this afternoon?'

'I'm sending out the letters to the subscribers,' Evelyn said and indicated the pile of sealed letters by the side of her machine.

'And I have been reading.'

'Excellent, excellent. All in order.' Pollack waved his hand. 'We shall have a staff conference.' He proceeded into his small inner office. Evelyn rose, taking her pad and pencil with her.

'Think about it, Julius,' she hissed at him as she followed Mr Pollack into his office. Julius went to his desk, picked up the play he had been reading, and followed.

Mr Pollack stepped out of his office into the adjoining small room. Julius and Evelyn settled themselves as they listened to the sound of Mr Pollack urinating. There was a token hiss of water in the sink, and Mr. Pollack came out, his fly still open, flitting his dampened hands in the air to dry them. Julius touched his fly to remind his employer. Mr Pollack gave a small look of surprise. 'Of course, of course, my boy. Excuse me, Evelyn,' he said gallantly as he carefully zipped his fly closed. 'Now,' he said, rubbing his hands together, 'we shall proceed to the first order of business.' He sat down briskly at his desk and stared out at Forty-eighth Street. They waited.

'I have been thinking –' Mr Pollack started as he looked out at the street, and then stopped. 'Well, never mind. For another time. For the moment, let's stick to what we have here.' He turned back to them and regarded them with a benign air. 'Every time I look at you both I say to myself: "Pollack, how lucky you are to have such a devoted and brilliant staff." Other theatrical producers are naked to the world and to their enemies. But I, Pollack, I have two loyal shield-bearers. They work restlessly for my good. Julius uncovers brilliant plays by totally unknown playwrights, and Evelyn crisply carries forward the myriad details connected with theatrical production. Other producers are wealthier and still others are more successful but what producer on Broadway is so well served? In the morning when I arise, I care for myself and my body and think throughout breakfast that when I arrive at my office my staff will have found something for me. Something unique, something astonishing, something to make Pollack a name to reckon with. Something to engage my soul, my creative instincts, my mind. Perhaps a new Shaw, a new Molnar, a new Strindberg – who knows? – perhaps even a new Shakespeare?' He chuckled wetly. 'It could happen. I don't know if I will live to see such good fortune. But it could happen. Now, let us have a report. First from

Julius, for it is his little department on which we turn such eager eyes. What bonbon, what little treasure have you for us, Julius?' Pollack leaned forward with a glittering look of tender expectancy.

'There is a play called' – Julius hastily consulted the cover of the manuscript – '*Love Is a Dry Summer*, by Lucien Cadwallader. I've finished two acts of it this morning.'

'Enchanting title,' Pollack said tossing his head with delighted astonishment. '*Love Is a Dry Summer*,' he repeated, and turned in his chair. 'I like the sound of it. Poetic and yet simple. Evocative and tender with yet a touch of harshness. What do you think, Evelyn?'

'I've read it. I think it's a bunch of Southern horse shit,' Evelyn said.

'A play placed in the Old South,' Pollack said thoughtfully.

'No, sir,' Julius said. 'It's placed in the modern South. Really Southwest. Or, at least, Arkansas. At least, I think it's Arkansas.'

'And what is the *raison d'être* of this work?' Pollack said.

Julius fidgeted. If he wanted to know the story, why didn't he ask? It wasn't fair to use foreign technical words on him. 'Well, it's about a mother and daughter living in this old house. And the mother is sort of mean to the daughter and the daughter is a sort of dreamer and then this young fellow, Roy, comes along and both the mother and the daughter fall in love with him and they both want him to stay but he can't. He has to leave.'

'He is a mysterious stranger, this young man, isn't he?' Pollack asked, his eyes narrowed. Julius was about to answer but Pollack went on. 'I see him now in my inner eye. He is young, splendid, unexplained, the Lochinvar out of the West.'

'No, he comes from Chicago,' Julius said, checking quickly.

Pollack waved his hand to brush off the fly of irrelevancy. 'He says little about himself. He is handy about the place, mending things. Saying little and yet the hungers in these two starved women mount as they watch him. He walks with assurance. Godlike assurance. And yet there is about his bright youth a haunted penumbra of evil. He will destroy these two women, for he is the flame and they are but two drugged, senseless moths, circling endlessly. One of them touches him and goes up into flames and the other, shocked, shrinks back from the final doom. Which is which?'

'That must be in the third act,' Julius said. 'I haven't read it.'

'Evelyn?'

'He lays both of them,' Evelyn said. 'Then he goes away. They both look forward to having babies for Christmas.'

'Wrong, wrong, all wrong,' Pollack said, waving his hands in the air. 'That must be rewritten at once. To leave the leading woman with a baby is all right. To leave the *ingénue* with a baby is all right. But to leave them both is bad theatre. It makes a farce.' Pollack suddenly brightened. 'Is it a farce?'

'There isn't a funny line in it,' Evelyn said grimly.

'No matter,' Pollack said. 'Farce is not really indigenous to the American theatre. We have the French farce. Have we heard from Paris?'

'Do you still want the Comédie-Française to do it?' Evelyn asked.

'But, of course!' Pollack said. 'Who else would do it? I will bring the whole company over.'

'But they don't speak English!' Evelyn protested.

'It would be remarkably curious if the Comédie-Française did,' Pollack explained with a gracious smile. 'Of course they will put it on in French.'

'And who's going to hold up the subtitles?' Evelyn asked acidly.

'Never mind. I will face the problems as they come. Theodore Pollack presents: *La Comédie-Française dans l'Homme de Moins*. I can see it most plainly. The mere announcement excites me. Begin with excitement and you will succeed. That is the axiom of the theatre. I am excited about this play Julius has found for us.'

He smiled gratefully at Pollack and forgot, for the moment, the sting of Evelyn's remarks. No talent, eh?

'Wire,' Pollack said crisply, 'the author's agent – name?'

'No agent,' Julius said. 'He sent it in himself. He's an assistant professor of drama at Oklahoma State University.'

'All the better. No one enjoys dealing with agents. Wire Mr – er –'

'Lucien Cadwallader, Department of Drama, Oklahoma State University, Enid, Oklahoma.'

'Have you got that?' Pollack asked. Evelyn nodded her head. 'Enchanted by your play – er – *Dry Summer* –'

'*Love Is a Dry Summer*,' Julius volunteered.

'*Love Is a Dry Summer*,' Pollack repeated. 'Not a title to forget. Enchanted by your play ... wire me earliest date you can be in New York to discuss minor revisions. Sign it, Theodore Pollack, and the address, of course.'

'I'll finish the play this afternoon, sir,' Julius said eagerly.

'No need to, my boy. It will all be changed after I have talked with the playwright. Well –' Pollack rubbed his hands together briskly – 'I must say – a satisfactory conference. A most satisfactory conference. Now, to your labours as I to mine. I am expecting a luncheon guest, Evelyn. A Mr Ryan.'

Evelyn nodded her head and rose. Before they left the room, Pollack had stretched himself out on the cracked leather sofa in his office and closed his eyes. They heard his snore through the thin partition a few moments later.

Julius went back to his desk, almost elated, and then he caught Evelyn's eyes through the thick lenses. 'Send it, Evelyn,' he said, suddenly caught up in pity and compassion for a man he had not seen.

'Don't be a fool,' Evelyn said evenly and went back to her typing. He crossed to her desk and leaned over.

'Send the telegram. Don't throw it away this time. Please, please.'

'Don't bother me,' she said and inexorably typed.

'Perhaps something will come of it. Pollack may —'

'You fool,' Evelyn said, shaking her head. 'No.'

'But perhaps this time —'

'Five years and you learn nothing,' she said and shook her head. 'It only takes four years to go through a university and you have spent five years here and you haven't learned anything yet.'

'But what if *this* time Pollack means it —'

The light caught Evelyn's lenses so that two white discs looked at him. 'This poor man is nearly two thousand miles away. Pollack sends a two-dollar telegram and goes to sleep. But think of what happens to him in Oklahoma. His hopes are raised, he shows the telegram to colleagues, to the university president, to friends, to enemies, to his wife, his children, his students. In his eyes he is on Broadway, the reviews written, the money in the bank, Hollywood on the telephone. Whatever little and big dreams he's got rush into life size. He has

Pollack's two-dollar message. He arranges for a leave of absence, spends money on bus fare to New York. Telephones us the moment he reaches the terminal. Within an hour he is here, waiting for Pollack. Pollack may or may not see him – perhaps for a week. They go to lunch. They discuss the play. Pollack has a hundred ideas, a thousand changes, Pollack holds out all kinds of titbits, a smell of Hollywood pastrami, a whiff of London production lox; he arranges national companies like toasted bagels. He drives the poor man wild with greed, with promises, and sends him home. The poor slob works and writes. Pollack writes back. I have written a thousand such letters. Pollack no longer composes them. I compose them. He signs them.'

'But he means to do well,' Julius protested.

'Pollack is a dreamer. A grave dreamer. I mean, he can dream people into their graves. When the summer comes, Pollack flits away from here. Where do you suppose he goes?'

'Summer stock,' Julius said.

'He goes to pontificate in hotels with dramatic directors. He wears a monocle with tinted glass. He speaks beautiful English to ladies. He lectures to housewives from Queens and Forest Hills and Long Island on the grass in front of the recreation building about drama. He supervises a production of a play and produces a thousand-dollar-a-week star for the discounted price of seven hundred fifty. For this he gets free lodgings, meals, laundry, all the drinks he wants, and eight hundred dollars at the end of the stay. This he does at five hotels for two weeks. He must live on that four thousand dollars the rest of the year. The money for this office, for your salary and mine, for the little expenses involved comes from his ex-wife, who can't stand him. I have an agreement with her. I am to keep the expenses down below a fixed figure. I get a percentage of the saving. Do you know why I am trying to discourage him from the Comédie-Française? Because I keep worrying the son of a bitch will pick up the phone and call Paris. In a week he could kill my budget with his calls to Paris. When I take this telegram and throw it in the wastebasket I save two dollars for Pollack's ex-wife and I save this college schnook a year of heartache.'

'But maybe this time –' Julius began. Evelyn shook her head.

'No.'

'Evelyn, have a heart –'

'I have a heart,' she said, looking up at him. 'I have a heart and that's why I say no. I care a little about what happens to human beings. Pollack doesn't care. Pollack lives in a dream world where people are daisies and he picks them out of the grass, admires them, kills them with the heat of his hand, and throws them away. Such a man is heartless because he is stupid. He doesn't look ahead. He is like a drunk driving on a highway, full of drunken skills and drunken airs. Behind him a litter of cripples and corpses and broken lives and tears and he goes sailing along and there is no policeman in sight to stop him. Well,' Evelyn said firmly, 'I am the policeman. I can't stop the man, but I can push a few innocents out of the way.'

'You are very unfair,' Julius said, sad for the professor in Oklahoma who would never feel the excitement of acceptance brush his soul.

Evelyn bent to her work. Julius returned to his desk and put aside Lucien Cadwallader's play with a sigh. He reached for another manuscript.

'You could become another Pollack,' Evelyn said after a while.

Julius looked up with surprise.

'Yes,' Evelyn said definitely, as though she had debated it with herself, 'you could, very easily. You don't
understand the meaning of truth, and people like you
are very dangerous.'

Her father was a hard, compact little man with square hands, square jaw, square eyebrows. He sat Julius down squarely on a chair and looked at him squarely.

'I don't understand what my daughter sees in you. I consider you a total imbecile.'

Julius cast a look of love at her. She looked back with a faint smile.

'I consider,' her father went on after he had taken Julius's chin between two fingers and moved his face so that it looked into the faded blue eyes, 'that you are a drugged, synthesized, adulterated, desexed product of your civilization.'

Julius bridled and was about to speak when her father held up a square, strong hand which looked powerful enough to break his face. Julius hesitated. One never knew what such nuts might do.

'I don't want to hear your voice,' her father said. 'It offends my ears. It offends my spirit. You are a human garbage pail into which radio and television have poured all of their slops. Give me the stupid courtesy you give these machines and remain silent and attentive.'

'I talk back at the television,' Julius said bravely.

'*Bravo*,' the girl said softly, and Julius glanced at her with gratitude.

Her father looked at him coldly. 'You are nearly demented, as well.'

Julius's soul curled a bit at the edges. Would nothing please this nut?

'You will, shortly, be in the company of your betters,' her father went on. 'These are men and women who, by contrast to you, are gods, living saints, prophets, messiahs. Nothing you can say is as important as what they say.'

'That's not democratic,' Julius countered.

'Democracy can only exist among men. Not men and cockroaches. You are a cockroach. Be silent when your betters speak.'

'I have rights,' Julius said stubbornly.

'Not here, not now,' her father replied. 'And do not insult me by offering to reply. I am not interested in your witlessness.' He rose then, glared menacingly at Julius, and walked out of the room.

When the door was closed he held out his hands and she came into his lap. Warm, soft, not too heavy. Perfect He sighed against her ear.

'Why doesn't he like me?' Julius asked, without genuine interest.

'He does,' she said. 'But he is ashamed for you. He is ashamed of what you are. What you have been made.' She kissed his cheeks and eyelids and forehead.

'Are you ashamed of me?'

'Of course,' she said dreamily as she put her hand inside his shirt.

'What?!' Julius said, suddenly startled.

She closed his mouth with hers and then opened them both and he felt the quickness of her tongue.

'That's an awful thing to say,' Julius said when he could speak.

'You can't help yourself,' she said mildly. 'You are what you are.'

'But you're satisfied with me, aren't you?' he asked hopefully.

'Oh, beautifully,' she said with a sensual smile, and worked her lips along his jaw to his ear.

'I don't mean that way,' he said, pushing her away slightly.

'Which way?' she asked.

'You know what I mean. *That* way.'

'Yes,' she said, leaning towards him, her lips opened, her eyes half closing. 'You are perfect. Sometimes almost as perfect as a girl.'

'What!?!' He cried out, and tried to stand up. She went to the floor. She sat on the floor, looking at him in bewilderment.

'Why did you do that?'

'You – you –' He shook his finger at her helplessly. 'You said a girl,' he finally managed to say, horrified.

'Well, why not? You find caressing a girl pleasant, don't you? Why shouldn't I?'

Julius swallowed hard. 'But you *are* a girl!'

She sat back, her weight on one stiffened arm, the calm blue eyes regarding him, the innocence of her mouth absolutely self-evident. 'I know. And I have caressed myself and I find that pleasant, too.'

Julius got up abruptly and began to pace the floor, deeply agitated, running his finger about inside of his collar. He was afraid to speak. Afraid to ask questions. How deep would it go?

'But that's wrong!' he cried out, looking at her in anguish. It was that goddamned nut of a father of hers. He raised her that way. He sat down on the couch and leaned forward. 'Those things are not *normal!*'

'Normal?' she asked.

'My God, weren't you ever told?'

'Who was supposed to tell me?'

Ah, there it was! That damned father of hers. 'Your mother,' he said quickly.

She thought a moment. 'My mother never told me.'

'Well, of course not!' he said heatedly. 'She probably didn't know what you were doing.'

'But I never kept it a secret,' she said.

'When – I mean – how long – I mean – where's your mother?'

'She went away with someone,' she said.

'When you were a little child,' Julius offered.

'No,' she said, shaking her head. 'Last summer. We expect her back soon. When she gets tired of him.'

'*Him?*' Julius asked with a soft shriek.

'She's never gone away with another woman,' she said thoughtfully. 'I suppose she doesn't see the pleasure in it.'

Julius shook his head and swallowed. He felt helpless. They weren't talking the same language. Why hadn't the police found out about them? Why weren't they all in jail? 'Please, please, listen to me,' he said, and knelt down on the floor beside her. 'There is something terribly wrong with your life.'

She moved closer to him so that her thigh touched his knees. She smiled at him radiantly, as a flower might smile at the raping bees. 'Tell me, Julius.'

'No, no. I mean listen – really listen to me.' He took her hand into his. 'What we did. That was natural. That was normal.' He steeled himself. 'But it wasn't right. It really wasn't right. We should have been married.'

'Do you want to get married?'

'What!'

'Do you want to be married to me?' she asked.

He got to his feet hastily. So that was her little game, eh? How damned clever. And see how she manoeuvred it. Ye gods! What cunning! What *finesse*. He circled her now. He was in better possession of himself. She was, of course, a liar. An accomplished liar. Other *girls*. Ha! Quite likely not! He smiled at her mysteriously.

'Why are you smiling, Julius?' she asked sweetly.

'You're very clever,' he said, the man of the world. He took out a cigarette, lit it, and blew a puff of smoke at the ceiling. This had to be handled properly. The little minx! She had Julius Schapiro on his knees but thank God for his quick, mother wit. He took out his cigarette and contemplated its smoke, his eyes narrowed. What a situation for Molnar! He would have to consider his words carefully. A silken approach on his part. 'You're very, *very* clever,' he said, and gave her his best second-act smile.

'How nice of you, Julius,' she said, following him with those candid blue eyes under the blond Dutch-girl haircut. 'Father doesn't consider me clever at all.'

'No,' he said, turning the cigarette in his hand with a mysterious smile. 'Your father wouldn't. Your *mother* would!' He clicked his teeth together. What a pregnant retort! He looked at her. There was still the innocent blankness in her eyes. Ha, ha. Not now. Not with him. He knew her better. The eternal Eve. The feminine witch. But the witch had met her match. *Witch, match. Oh, witch with the golden eyeees! Oh, witch with the gooolden hair! I'm your match, you witchhhh. You've enchanted meeee! Enchanted, enchanted, enchanted meee! Now set me freeeee! Oh, watch me witch.*

'Are you singing to yourself?' she asked.

'No, no,' Julius said quickly, catching himself. Close thing. He would have to remember the rhyme scheme. Lots of potential there.

'You make up songs about everything, don't you?' she asked.

Julius suddenly felt embarrassed, as though someone had poured hot water into his drawers. 'Don't be a little fool!' he snapped, trying to regain the Molnar touch. 'I was thinking what it would be like being your husband.'

Not a good Molnar line, but it would lead to better.

'Would you want very many children?'

What a nasty sense of practicality she had! If all the Molnar lines were going to be his, she would have to do better. 'I think a discussion about children premature,' he said loftily. Not top-hole Molnar but with a glimmer.

'I am not sure I want to marry you,' she said thoughtfully.

Julius's eyes opened in surprise. What a gambit! What singleness of purpose! How quick she was on her conversational feet! On her butt she moves faster than you, Schapiro! He regarded the cigarette. It was getting shorter now and as a prop it was burning itself out. Nothing for it but to snub it out in the ash tray. He looked about. No ash tray in sight. Wouldn't you know it?

'I don't want to be a swine, my dear,' he said, holding the burning cigarette upward like a small smoking birthday candle, 'but is it very clear that I want to marry you?' *Touché!* Definitely first-class Molnar! He edged the cigarette away from his fingers. They were beginning to feel its heat.

'But why shouldn't you want to marry me?' she asked, and looked at him. 'I'm young and pretty and I satisfy you sexually and I am healthy and I would bear straight, handsome, healthy children. I can cook and clean —' she stopped. 'Isn't that cigarette burning your fingers?'

'No, not at all,' he grimaced and could happily have kicked her. He turned towards the windows and tried spitting on the cigarette to put it out. His efforts merely fanned the coal to burn the remaining quarter-inch even faster. He was in an agony. He gathered a huge glob of spittle for one final, all-out desperate bombing attempt. He sighted carefully, and as he opened his mouth to let the spittle out, her father opened the door abruptly, startling him. He turned, his face screwed up in pain, a blob of spittle hanging idiotically from his lower lip. Her father regarded him furiously as the spittle fell to the rug.

'I think people who spit indoors are beneath contempt,' her father said.

Julius crushed out the glowing coal between his fingers and smothered the scream of pain that rushed to his top story and hammered at his tongue.

'Are you ready?' her father asked, getting into a curiously European leather jacket.

'Yes,' she said, springing up gracefully.

Her father marched out of the house putting a leather workman's cap on his head. She hurried over with his coat and helped him into it. He cramped his wounded hand.

Did you hurt yourself?' she asked.

He shook his head bravely, his eyes swimming in pain.

'Why did you spit on the floor?' she asked as they started out the door. A glob of shame filled his skull and made his nose run and he wished with great intensity that he was dead, dead, dead.

The secretary read the minutes. She was a huge woman with iron-grey hair and granitic features and a voice filled with gutturals, clicks, hisses and pops. She wore a pince-nez with a silver chain, and now and then poised her hand on the continental shelf below her chins. A massive corset had made of both her belly and her breasts one immense promontory fit to set against an ocean.

The other gods and messiahs and prophets and living saints were scattered about on battered chairs. A large soft man who sighed and looked about with sad eyes, an angry coarse man with spiky hair and noisy shoes, which he scraped and scratched against the wooden floor. Julius held his injured hand cupped, feeling the throbbing of the twin blisters. A thin slat of a woman with hair drawn back neatly in an artificial-looking bun sat in front of him. She made notes with a large crayon in a children's schoolbook. The girl's father sat in his chair as chairman. A young man with a beard, reminiscent of President Benjamin Harrison, smoked incessantly and kept a conversation, in a low tone, going with a girl who wore long black cotton stockings and a good deal of Mexican silver costume jewellery.

In the midst of the minutes, the man with the noisy shoes and the spiky hair suddenly stood up. 'Why do we have to have all this bull about minutes!'

The girl's father looked at the dissenting messiah with the same calm blue eyes. 'The Truth Seekers must adhere to certain disciplines. To seek the truth without discipline is to invite anarchy.'

'What's wrong with anarchy?' the young President Benjamin Harrison asked, breaking off his conversation with the girl in the long black cotton stockings.

'I am using the term "anarchy" in its literary sense rather than in its political or philosophical sense,' her father said evenly.

'I just want it understood that anarchy is not to be run down here,' the young man with the beard said.

'I defer to your learned opinion,' her father said almost sweetly.

'I'm still against the minutes,' the man with the noisy shoes said.

'The secretary will note the speaker's objection and conclude.'

The secretary took an immense breath and finished rapidly.

The fat man of sighs waved a pudgy hand. 'Mr Chairman. Do I see a new Truth Seeker with us tonight?'

Julius felt their eyes turn towards him. He shrank back in his chair. She put her hand on his thigh, and he shrank back from that.

'The gentleman is not yet a Truth Seeker,' her father said grimly. 'I consider him a poor prospect.'

The thin slat of a woman with the bun turned and fixed her eyes on Julius. 'Then,' she said in a clear, piercing voice, 'do I understand that he is here to mock us?'

'No, no,' Julius said quickly in a small voice.

'Is he a writer?' the young man with the presidential beard said, rising to see Julius more clearly.

'A song writer,' Julius volunteered hesitantly. His answer was greeted by a series of barks and snorts.

'Do you know what I think of your songs?' the man with the noisy shoes said, rising with an air of menace.

'I think they're all crap!' He came across the floor and close to Julius, who shrank back in his chair. He put his face close to Julius's. 'Crap!' he exploded, and the spittle struck Julius's cheek.

'There is no doubt,' the large soft sighing man said, 'that popular American music is a debased form of art.'

'I say it's crap!' the man with the spiky hair said ringingly.

'A trap, a snare, a delusion,' the thin slat of a woman said in an odd singsong, her eyes fixed on Julius.

'That does not mean that progressive jazz is part of American music,' the young bearded man said. 'I find in it strong elements of the dissident, the outsider, the breaking away from the traditional patterns of music, a new exploration of the truth in music.' The young man fingered his beard. 'Why haven't you broken the patterns in music?'

'I want to sell my songs,' Julius said.

'Let him sing one of his songs,' the large soft man said.

'What for?' the spiky-haired man said. 'We all know it's going to be a lot of crap!'

'Let's be fair,' the large soft man said. 'Perhaps he has found the truth in his songs.'

'Do your songs rhyme?' the thin slat of a woman asked.

'Of course,' Julius said. 'All songs rhyme.'

'What did I tell you?' the spiky-haired man cried triumphantly.

'What are the subjects of your songs?' the young bearded saint asked.

'Love.'

'Hopeless,' the thin slat of a woman said, and turned away.

The secretary looked at him carefully. 'Why are you here?'

'Because I was invited by this young lady.'

All eyes turned towards the girl. She smiled at them sweetly, proudly. 'He makes up songs all the time. I think he's making up one right now. Aren't you, Julius?'

He shook his head in agony. 'No, no, no.'

The large soft man said, 'We could use a song just for ourselves.'

'We have a song,' the young bearded man said. 'It is here.' He tapped his skull. 'It is a song without music, without words. It is the purest music, the cleanest words. I wouldn't dirty my mouth with the words he's likely to write. I wouldn't clog my ears with the sounds he thinks are music.'

'That's it,' the spiky-haired man said. 'Tell the son of a bitch off!'

The young bearded man was on his feet. 'We are an army without banners, a host without drums or bands. We are the friendless, the despised, the aliens, the ones scoffed and mocked. We are the nonconformists. the loners, the people with a dream in their eyes and a belly filled with last night's beans. We're on the road, homeless, rootless, the bums of a thousand cities, the tramps of ten thousand roads, the hoboes of the garbage heap they call American civilization. We're the Truth Seekers. Why? Because we live in an age of sham and hypocrisy and lies and swindles and frauds and bunco games, and the welter of cheating and stealing and lying has sickened us so that we have to climb out of it and cleanse ourselves. I tell you, when I come here I feel clean for the first time in my life. I feel as though I have peeled the scum of the world from my skin when I first step into this room. This is my woman.' He touched the shoulder of the girl with the black cotton stockings and the Mexican silver jewellery. 'I live with her. I sleep with her and I am not married to her.'

'Aw, never mind that crap!' the spiky-haired man said, and fidgeted in his seat noisily.

'We live as Nature intended us to live,' the young bearded messiah went on, ignoring the rude interruption. 'As man and woman – without the hypocrisy of state sanction. We take each other naked and free –' Julius noticed that the girl was pulling on the young man's sleeve urgently. 'Without any thought –' The pulling became more urgent and the girl's voice was a sharp hiss. 'I'm not ashamed,' he declared, looking down at the girl. 'I wouldn't be ashamed to do it right here – where we're all clean –'

'I don't think there's any need for that!' the thin slat of a woman said sharply.

'But if we're seeking the truth –' the young bearded man said.

The large soft man surprisingly giggled and then put his hand to his mouth as if he had lapsed socially.

'Jesus Christ,' Julius said softly, and looked at his girl. She smiled at him mysteriously.

'Well, damn it,' the young bearded prophet said, 'if you're going to be a bunch of prudes about it, I *will* do it!'

The girl with the black cotton stockings got up quickly and scampered out of the room, slamming the door sharply behind her.

'While I like to allow the Truth Seekers the greatest amount of freedom in their discussion and action,' the chairman said gravely, 'I don't feel that the honourable speaker's intention will do anything to further our cause.'

'Now, just a minute,' the young bearded man said. 'It certainly will. Don't you know the crippling effect prudery has on our country? I'll say, without fear of contradiction, that the mass lies about sex, the cheap, sniggering superstructure of morality about sex has done more to maim and wound us as human beings than any one element in our culture. If we're seeking the truth, as we're always saying we are, then let's seek it without fear or false modesty. What is sex but the coming together of a man and a woman? Never mind all the faking and foppishness and foolishness. A man and a woman. I'm ready – here and now – to prove to you that there is nothing shameful in it, nothing to snigger at, nothing to giggle over. Who will seek the truth with me – here and now? Who will put the lie of sex to death here in our place of truth in this moment of truth?' He looked about as they all looked at one another. Julius looked at his girl and suddenly seized her hand when he saw a dreamy, speculative look swim into her eyes.

'Aw, what is all this?' the spiky-haired man said uncomfortably, forgetting his favourite epithet in his embarrassment.

'Really, must we have it right here at this moment?' the large soft man said, opening and closing his hands uncomfortably.

'Yes, now! Here! Who will seek the truth with me?' the young bearded man cried out. The thin slat of a woman pressed her crayon hard against the copybook, and Julius hung on to his girl's hand with a fierce unrelenting grip.

There was a groan of furniture as the secretary, her pince-nez shaking on the bridge of her nose, heaved her bulk upward. 'I will! Here I am!' She threw up her short massive arms as one importunes Heaven. The young bearded man quailed for a moment, and his shoulders moved inward with a wince.

'He was hoping for you,' Julius said in a low hissing

tone. She looked at him obliquely out of her blue eyes and smiled.

The Truth Seekers regarded the secretary, her hands opened to the Heavens, her eyes closed behind the pince-nez. The young bearded man hesitated, his eyes rooted on the secretary. His horror floated restlessly in the air about him until even Julius, sitting in the back of the room, could smell the odour of decayed cheese. It would be only instants before it reached the enraptured volunteer's nose.

'Serves you right!' the spiky-haired man said meanly.

The chairman, staring ahead with honest blue eyes, began to tug on the secretary's skirt. She did not feel the pulling through her layers of corset for a moment or so and then she opened her eyes, watching for her slender despoiler.

'Sit down,' her father said in a voice so small and strangled that Julius's heart suddenly leaped across the room to comfort the man.

The secretary looked about bewildered and sat down heavily, her promontory heaving with excitement or frustration or shame or all three. She fixed her eyes on the papers in front of her.

The slender bearded man wrung his hands and then quickly turned and walked out of the room, closing the door softly behind him.

'We will,' the chairman said, clearing his throat, 'proceed to the next order of business. One of the Truth Seekers has complained concerning the advertising of a motion picture. The Truth Seeker declares that he paid one dollar and ninety cents to see the picture and the advertising was fraudulent. A letter of protest has been drafted for transmission to the management of the theatre. Similarly, letters have been prepared for transmission to the producers of the motion picture, the

Mayor of the City of New York, the Governor of the State of New York, the Governor of the State of California, where the picture was manufactured, the Mayor of the City of Los Angeles, the place of manufacture, and, of course, the usual copy to the President of the United States and to the Secretary-General of the United Nations for his information. I propose to read the letter to you for your approval.'

Julius's jaw hung slack. The *President* of the United States? Over a lousy dollar ninety?

Mysterious, electromagnetic waves of love radiated from the kitchen. They moved through the walls of the apartment and struck the solid figure sitting at the table eating. Equally mysterious impulses bounced back and registered on the radar screen of Mrs Schapiro's brain. The fine, clean ping of response satisfied her and she exhaled with quiet joy. Her short, fat, varicosed legs trembled with pleasure. Julius was home. Julius was eating. All's right with the world.

She moved into the dining-room to satisfy her eyes as well. Julius was home. Julius was eating. A subject fit for a painting. A hand painting.

'Well, darling,' she said, lingering over the endearment, her fingers curving with the desire to touch his dear head. 'Is it good?'

'Delicious, Ma,' Julius said.

'Make noise when you eat the soup. Then I'll know you are enjoying.' She placed her body into a chair.

'It isn't polite to make noise when one eats, Ma,' Julius said, dropping *mandelin* into his soup.

Mrs Schapiro shook her head. Such brilliance! And he never went to college! 'And how is work?'

'Oh, it's fine.'

'Mr Pollack is happy with you?' It was a purely rhetorical question. Who cared what that dried-up nothing Pollack thought of her child! As if Pollack, with his skinny old man's behind and his fool's eyes and fop's manners and questionable moral background, mattered in the world! What was Pollack? A nothing, a cipher, a boor, a cow, an incurable aneuretic, a woman chaser, with his ridiculous walking stick! Was he fit to judge her gilded son? Was he fit to judge even the degree of dirt in the street? What was he, after all? A nonentity!

'Mr Pollack has been very pleased with me, Ma,' Julius said. 'I found a play for him recently from a fellow who lives in Brooklyn. It's called *The Morning I Die*, by Seymour Waxler.

'Wexler?'

'Waxler,' Julius said.

Mrs. Schapiro's homemade programmer and computer sifted a thousand names. 'I used to know a family named Wachsberg.'

'Waxler.'

'Or maybe it was Wachsman,' she said, the tiny, uneven relays of her mind stuttering. 'What was his mother's maiden name?'

'Gosh, Ma, I don't know that. That's not on the manuscript.'

'You'll find out, Julius,' his mother said, edging forward the boiled chicken. 'It seems to me I know the family.'

'Waxler?'

'Let me know her maiden name. I used to know a woman who married a man in Brooklyn. A second marriage. Her first husband was carried away. She married a man named Wachstein.'

'But his name is Waxler,' Julius said, pulling the boiled chicken towards him.

'Let me know her maiden name,' Mrs Schapiro said with mystical confidence.

Julius looked at his mother. She had mysterious powers for making things come out when they seemed unlikely. She took string that never looked long enough and made it fit. She could foretell the weather better than the United States Weather Bureau, with all of its meteorological aids. For the elemental, primal things in life, his mother was a kind of genius who never ceased to amaze him. She would find the thread of acquaintance which would lead to Seymour Waxler one way or the other.

'So, Mr Pollack is happy with you? And when is Evelyn getting married?'

'Gosh, I don't know, Ma,' Julius said. 'Maybe she's given up.'

'They never give up,' Mrs Schapiro said with light-hearted anger. 'When they put them away they bend a little finger to the gravedigger. Don't let her get too friendly, Julius.'

'She wouldn't be interested in me, Ma,' Julius protested.

Mrs Schapiro smiled mysteriously. 'Eat, Julius, eat.'

'But, Ma, seriously – you can't mean that – Evelyn is over forty!'

'Maybe she's closer to fifty?' Mrs Schapiro asked archly.

Julius debated it for a moment and shook his head. 'No, she's not that old, Ma. I'm sure she's not more than forty-one!'

'I wish I had a dollar for every year she's over that!' Mrs Schapiro sang tonelessly.

'Gee, Ma,' Julius said, 'don't you like Evelyn?'

'*I* don't like Evelyn?' Mrs Schapiro cried with an air of deep affront, her hand on her bosom. 'Julius, you should be ashamed!'

'But the way you talk –'

'So I discussed her true age! Does that mean I don't

like her? I think she's a fine woman. A fine woman. Where would that office be without her? What would happen to Mr Pollack if she wasn't there, hunh? Could he wipe his behind without Evelyn? She runs that corporation.' Mrs Schapiro moved the tines of a fork delicately among a few bread crumbs and added with quiet malice, 'In more ways than one.'

'You can say that again!' Julius said vigorously as he attacked the boiled chicken.

'You saw something?' Mrs Schapiro asked quickly, her prurience and her alarm awakened in the same bed by a sudden noise.

'No. Evelyn told me.'

'Told you what?' Mrs Schapiro asked, trying to conceal her eagerness.

'Well, it's a business matter,' Julius said, feeling that ethics prevented him from speaking.

'Oh, business,' Mrs Schapiro said, disappointed prurience falling back into bed and alarm yawning. But curiosity, with its head filled with eyes and random ears, was awake. 'What kind of business?'

'Oh, Mr Pollack's ex-wife pays for running the office.'

'That,' Mrs Schapiro said with deep boredom, 'I figured out for myself a long time ago.'

'No kidding?' Julius asked, looking at his mother with pride and astonishment.

'A business is a business, Julius,' Mrs Schapiro said. 'Even when they call it show business. All I see in Pollack's business is merchandise coming and going and people drawing salaries but nobody's buying anything. Rent costs money, electric costs money, telephone calls cost money, you and Evelyn cost money, the janitor has to get Christmas presents, the window washer costs money, pencils and paper cost money. So far in Pollack's business all I see are costs. Where are the sales? Where's the income? It has to come from some place. Pollack is not a rich man. So where? He's too old to have rich parents. So he gets it from his wife.'

'Elementary, my dear Watson,' Julius said, downing nearly a full glass of charged water. He glanced at his wrist watch.

The glance did not escape Mrs Schapiro, nor her count. By count, it was the fourth time he had looked at his watch. 'There's a special show on television tonight?' she asked innocently.

'No, Ma, not so far as I know.'

'You had your watch fixed today?'

'No,' Julius said, puzzled.

'You keep looking at it to see if it's running.'

'Oh, I've got a d— appointment later.'

Mrs Schapiro sat silent for a long moment. There was no doubt about it in her mind. Her son was about to say 'date' when he changed the word to 'appointment'. Now a young man could have a meeting arranged to meet another young man and use the word 'date'. That was not usual but Julius had friends and he made dates with them sometimes. To go bowling, to go to a motion-picture show, to go to the theatre, to go for a drive. Appointments were another thing. Appointments were for business, to see a song publisher, to transact business, to prepare to transact business. Sometimes a young man meant to say appointment and said date instead. But when he had a date and changed his mind to call it an appointment then it was not a date with one of his friends. It was a date. And a date meant a girl. Mrs Schapiro's linguistic and semantic analysis was over in a split second. She considered another split second the thousand ways of finding out about the girl and decided to plunge full ahead.

'Julius, are you seeing a girl?'

Julius paused for an instant, his fork half-way to his mouth. The pause and the posture sent a pang to Mrs Schapiro's heart. *Oi veh!* It was even worse than she thought. 'Sort of, Ma.'

'So what's her name?'

Julius paused for a moment, trapped. He grinned. 'I don't know.'

Mrs Schapiro smiled. But under her smile a chasm yawned hideously dark, empty, bottomless. 'So what's her name?'

'I mean it, Ma. I don't really know her first name. Her last name is Leydecker.'

'That's a funny name,' Mrs Schapiro said with a smile. The doors of her house were torn off the hinges and the mob, multi-headed, hydra-tongued, teeth glinting here and there, waited for her Julius. She knew, whatever she did not know, that there wasn't a Jew in the crowd. There was, whatever else she did not know, the family Leydecker with their scrawny, underfed, ill-natured, stupid, greedy, vacant-eyed daughter. They were crying out, in some god-awful tongue, 'We're here for the wedding! The wedding!' And she looked out at the darkness, and the Leydeckers called out, 'We brought her relatives, too.'

'It's not so funny,' Julius said calmly.

'Jewish it's not,' Mrs Schapiro said with a smile that was meant to be ingratiating.

'Oh, I'm not so sure,' Julius said vaguely.

Mrs Schapiro waited, confident now that the mob, whatever gypsies, thugs, vagabonds, drunkards and wastrels they were, they were not Jewish. About a Jew, one is not unsure. A jew is a jew and a jew knew a jew. As her younger sister Sally used to say, from the motion picture of the same name. 'German, maybe,' Mrs Schapiro said helpfully with an unspoken curse.

'After all, they're Americans,' Julius reminded her.

'So's the Chinaman in the laundry,' Mrs Schapiro thought bitterly. Maybe you'd like to marry his daughter. Better yet the Chinaman. He was the only goy she knew who didn't hate Jews. He hated people without tickets. Why not a nice coloured girl? 'So they are Americans. Indians, maybe?' Mrs Schapiro said gaily.

Julius smiled at his mother. 'Ah, come on, Ma. She's a very nice girl.' He paused. 'But she's got troubles.'

Not as many troubles as I'll give her crooked little bones, Mrs Schapiro thought grimly. 'So you feel sorry for her?'

'Well, yes, I do. And then again, she wasn't raised properly.'

Never mind how she was raised. I'll lower her myself, into her grave. I'm starting to save for her headstone tonight. You'll be the youngest widower in the East Bronx, my dear Julius. 'Her parents are living?' Mrs Schapiro asked cheerfully.

'Yes, they are,' Julius said.

More good news, my son. 'That's nice,' Mrs Schapiro said. 'Her father is working?'

'I suppose so,' Julius said abstractedly.

Before you support them, my son, I'll have them committed to the old people's home. 'A professional man?' Mrs Schapiro asked. What a foolish question! Since when was collecting garbage a profession? A garbage man he's got to be. Or at least a janitor. Names like Leydecker you always saw over the janitor's mailbox. Names like Goldberg, Cohen, Lapidus, Schwartz, were tenants. Leydecker was never a tenant. He was a janitor and a lousy janitor at that. He threw coal into the furnace one piece at a time. Leydecker, I know you. I know you from a hundred apartments from the Bronx and Brooklyn. I know your tribe and may they rot. You let floods form in kitchens before you come to fix the pipe. You mop the floors with a dirty rag of a mop. You are stingy with coal and greedy for presents. You chip brand-new baby carriages in the basement because you haven't the courage to bash in the brains of Jewish babies. You get drunk in your rat's nest of an apartment and curse the Jews who are your betters, including the Jewish landlord who hired you. And you are going to be my son's father-in-law? When bells grow on the Pope's behind you'll be his father-in-law! This is Schapiro talking.

'Well, I don't know exactly what he does. I think he's a cabinetmaker,' Julius said.

'Well, at least he has a trade,' Mrs Schapiro said generously. May he saw off all of his fingers on his next job! I'll make him a cabinet, this cabinetmaker. Big enough for him and his wife and his daughter. On a nice plot some place. Overlooking a highway. Inside a cemetery.

'He's a Truth Seeker,' Julius added as he reached for his apple-sauce.

'He's not a citizen?' Mrs Schapiro asked, thrown into confusion.

'No, no, I mean he belongs to an organization that's looking for the truth,' Julius said. 'They're very unusual people.'

Ah, hah! I'm writing to the FBI tonight. Communists they've got to be, at the very least. They should get nice long sentences. Dear God, give them a mean judge. Not a soft-hearted Italian or a good-natured Jew but a mean son of a bitch of an Irishman with a red nose and a red neck. And let them go to dirty jails. Where they have to wear an iron ball on their legs. 'They sound like maybe they're radicals,' Mrs Schapiro said with a faint laugh.

'Gosh, Ma, I don't think so,' Julius said thoughtfully as he spooned up the apple-sauce. 'They were talking about writing to governors and to the President of the United States. But they were complaining about a movie.'

'The President of the United States. Oh, my, oh my,' Mrs Schapiro said. A long jail sentence it's got to be. To bother the President of the United States over a motion picture means jail definitely. The nerve of those janitors! Better they should give heat in the winter and service. No, they have to write and complain about the movies. And why? Why? It's plain as anyone can see. Because the movies are owned by Jews and they hate the Jews. Who do they think they're fooling? A dumb goy like the President of the United States they might fool. But not Schapiro. Schapiro knows what they are *really* complaining about. Tonight Schapiro writes to J. Edgar Hoover. A fine family you want to marry into, my son. Jailbirds. Jew-haters, radicals. Janitors.

Julius finished his apple-sauce. 'It was a delicious dinner, Ma. I've got to run.' He rose and pecked at her cheek.

Mrs Schapiro stayed at the table. When he was getting into his coat, she asked, 'Julius, where is the writing paper and the ink?'

'You'll find some in my desk, Ma. Writing to someone?'

'Yes, a little note,' Mrs Schapiro said, pursing her lips. 'I want to let them in on a bargain.'

'You and your bargains, Ma,' Julius said tenderly, shaking his head.

No, my darling son, you and *your* bargains! I'll make such bargains of them that Hitler won't have them. 'You should wear a hat at night,' Mrs Schapiro said to Julius.

'Gee, Ma, I hate hats.'

'It's not healthy to go in the night-time without a hat,' Mrs Schapiro said. When the janitor's daughter is taking care of you, you won't need a hat. An old silk stocking you can wear as a hat then. Good for taking out the ashes. Her ashes. Julius, if you marry her, I'll give a wedding present you'll never forget. A dead mother.

The author of *The Morning I Die*, in three acts and twelve scenes, was a short, hairy young man from Brooklyn. Hair, in fact, was his predominating physical characteristic. It grew from his head, his ears, his nose, from beneath his collar, at his wrists, peeking from the space between the elastic ends of his socklets and his trousers. He had a large nose, a determined jaw, and small, yellow-brown eyes. He carried a new attaché case of genuine imitation Fabrikoid. Julius had admired the same case in Liggett's Drug Store. It sold for seven ninety-eight.

Evelyn disliked him from the moment she saw him. He was there to have a luncheon appointment with Pollack to discuss his play. Julius could not keep his eyes off the visitor. He admired Mr Seymour Waxler. There was such fire, such passion in his play. It was the story of a beautiful schoolteacher, in her early fifties, who ran off with one of her high-school students. There were wonderful scenes in which the teacher faced the scorn and surprise and indignation of her colleagues, her relatives, her friends, and equally wonderful scenes in which the student stood off the cries and imprecations of his parents, the sneers of his friends. Julius had highly recommended the play to Pollack. In fact, he felt more strongly about Mr Waxler's play than he had felt about Mr Cadwallader's play, so that his disappointment over the Southern play was forgotten in his excitement over this one. And, too, as Evelyn had pointed out when she sent the wire, 'How much can he lose? Car-fare from Brooklyn?'

Evelyn typed her letters, now and again looking at Pollack's new playwright. Lunch. Imagine wasting money on that. It would be cheaper to take him to a fruit stand and let him eat a coconut or two and give him a stalk of bananas. Married, too. Imagine. It must be like going to bed with a fur coat. A cheap fur coat. Before I give Pollack lunch money, I want to hear it talk. So far nothing but grunts. Maybe it's an escaped ape who murdered the real Seymour Waxler and is masquerading. Who knew what went on in the minds of apes? Now it's going to smoke. This ought to be a good trick.

Seymour Waxler carefully filled a new meerschaum (imitation) pipe with shag tobacco (genuine) from an oil-skin (synthetic) pouch. He lit the pipe with a kitchen match (genuine).

Julius watched the pipe-lighting with pleasure. He admired the pipe, the deep graceful Sherlock Holmes curve and the large white bowl. Some people had style. Pollack had style. Seymour Waxler had style. Julius wondered wistfully if he had style.

Pollack entered. He wore, this morning, a chesterfield with a frayed velvet collar. The Homburg, as usual, the walking stick, as usual.

'Good morning, good morning,' Pollack sang out, and because he had a visitor he sailed directly past the clothes tree for his office.

Seymour Waxler had no opportunity to rise. Pollack, the old broken-field runner, was too quick for him. In and out, the door shut while the hand was reaching for the pipe and the legs beginning to straighten.

The inter-communication box scratched into life. Pollack, safe in his office: 'Evelyn, how is my call to Paris?'

'The transatlantic circuits are busy,' Evelyn said. They had been busy for three days, according to Evelyn. A fact which did not dismay Pollack. He was prepared to wait. Evelyn was prepared to keep him waiting.

'Well, keep after it, keep after it. Will you please come in for a brief conference and ask Mr Schapiro to step in, too?'

'Yes, Mr Pollack,' Evelyn said, rising. Julius picked up Mr Waxler's play, hesitating long enough with it so that Waxler should know. The new Ibsen from Brooklyn appeared to pay no attention. He began thumbing through an old copy of *Theatre Arts*.

As they entered, the toilet flushed, the hiss of water in the sink followed, and as a grand conclusion of the sequence, Pollack entered with a smile, fly opened.

'The hairy ape outside claims to be Seymour Waxler,' Evelyn said, and touched her lap to remind Pollack. Pollack, with a little flustered smile, almost lovingly closed the zipper.

'Waxler?'

'*The Morning I Die*,' Julius reminded him and held up the playscript.

'Oh, yes, yes, of course.'

'You're taking him to lunch,' Evelyn said accusingly.

'Yes, of course. Julius will come along too,' Pollack said.

Evelyn's mouth clamped shut in disapproval.

Julius was about to reply that he had brought his lunch from home but kept still. He loved to go to lunch with Pollack. It only happened two or three times a year. Yet he knew that Evelyn disaproved, and what was he to do with his sandwiches and the fruit? It hurt him to throw away food. It was sinful.

'Evelyn, please call Sardi's and reserve a table.'

'Why Sardi's?' Evelyn protested. 'Wouldn't you be happier at a small French restaurant?'

'Yes, I would,' Pollack said and sighed, 'but when in

the theatre give the profession its due. He will like Sardi's. Playwrights expect it.'

'Writing a play doesn't make a playwright,' Evelyn said dryly.

'Ah, Evelyn, Evelyn, you wonderful creature,' Pollack said with sweet sadness. 'I will need some money from petty cash. Fifty, I think, ought to take care of it.'

'I can give you twenty,' Evelyn said, rising.

'Show the young man in, Evelyn. I'd like to see him alone for a few moments before we leave. You won't mind, Julius, will you?'

'Oh, not at all sir,' Julius said, rising hastily.

When Seymour Waxler had entered Pollack's office, Evelyn telephoned Sardi's, made the reservation, and then hanged down the receiver, 'Sardi's! Julius!'

'Yes, Evelyn?'

Evelyn opened her purse and took out two ten-dollar bills. 'I am giving you twenty dollars to pay the tab at Sardi's. You grab the tab, you pay it. You will leave precisely fifteen per cent of the tab, without including the drinks, as the tip. You will not order a drink for yourself. You will eat the cheapest thing on the menu. No dessert.'

'Yes, Evelyn,' Julius said earnestly, trying to keep the details straight.

'You will *not* tip the checkroom girl a quarter. Collect all the coats and attaché cases and pipes and canes on one check. Give her a half-dollar for the whole equipage and never mind her dirty looks. No tip for the wine steward, even if he does a *kazotsky* with a flaming sword on your table. You will buy your cigarettes *before* you go in. Pollack won't be hungry, so I'm not worried about him. You're not supposed to be hungry on the office's money, so I'm not worried about you. I'm worried about the gorilla. Encourage him to eat bread and butter and water, water, lots of water. Keep asking for fresh rolls and more butter and don't forget the water.'

'Yes, Evelyn,' Julius said, and took the two bills and carefully put them inside his wallet, separating his own money from it, first. 'I have some sandwiches and fruit my mother gave me for lunch. Would you like to have them?' Julius asked.

'I'm on a diet,' Evelyn said, and when she saw the dismay in Julius's face she added, 'Well, leave them. Maybe an actor will come in. God only knows why anyone would want to keep an actor alive, but I'm big-hearted.'

'You are,' Julius agreed soberly.

Evelyn looked at him quickly and then smiled oddly. 'Julius, to see you walking around is to feel that you represent a waste of criminal size. Consider how many clean-cut, well-educated, healthy, employed, single girls there are. They brush their hair, they disinfect their mouths with peppermint rinses, they scour their teeth, they take vitamins, they starve their bellies to keep their figures, they take sun-lamp treatments, and they polish their poops. And they don't know about you. They dream about you, they talk about you, and yet they don't see you. And why not? Because they keep looking at blown-up images of men who live in Los Angeles California on the movie screen. They look at little images of men on television picture tubes. They look at pictures of men in magazines. They never look at the men about them. They'll look at the man on another girl's arm, after they've looked the girl over. They'll look at him. But not at you. Why not at you, I wonder? Because they're all equipped with X-ray eyes. They look through real things to see dead things. They don't see tissues. They see only bones. They look through you because you're like a tie on a pushcart. You can have one for nineteen cents. How good can it be?' She shook her head. 'Silly, silly girls. Julius, you are a gem. With a little flaw, to be sure. But how perfect are the girls? How perfect are these princesses of Ohrbach's and Macy's? Julius, if I weren't old enough to be your goddamned mother, I'd snap you out of circulation and make something of you.'

He smiled. 'My mother says you might be trying to do that anyway.'

Evelyn turned a steady sober gaze on him. 'Julius, I've only met your mother twice in five years. In any case, I didn't speak to her for more than ten minutes each time. But I know her right down to her little hammer toes. Your mother is a triple-plyed monster of the old school of Jewish monsters. She's not a mother. She's a growth. You grew on her twenty-four years ago and for one intolerable moment an interfering stranger cut you apart. She has been growing on you ever since. Such mothers should, on the birth of their children, be given a bouquet of flowers and two bullets in the brain.'

'Evelyn!' Julius said horrified.

'Now you know why I'm not married,' Evelyn said. 'No man has ever taken me home to his mother when she didn't guess the minute my foot touched her waxed floor that I hated her.'

'I wouldn't let the fact that my mother didn't like the girl keep me from marrying her,' Julius said sturdily.

'Spoken like a sleep-walker,' Evelyn said.

'Why does everyone call me a sleep-walker?' he asked petulantly.

'Because you are,' Evelyn said sadly. 'God only knows what might happen to you if you awoke. You might go out of your mind. You might become a man.'

Pollack and Seymour Waxler came out.

'Go, go to lunch,' Evelyn said quickly in a lowered

voice. 'Forget what I said. Eat a lot. Have dessert. Have two desserts. The bitch can afford it.'

Julius took his hat and coat and followed Pollack out.

When they arrived at the restaurant, Pollack made a fuss over the table. They had to change their table three times. First because it was too far from the door, then because it was in a draught, and finally because it afforded a poor view of the other diners.

'It is always best to dine where one is known,' Pollack finally said. 'Life is too brief to be unhappy even for a moment when it comes to creature comfort. Don't you agree, Seymour?'

'Personally,' Seymour Waxler began, and cleared his throat noisily, 'I don't care much about petty things like creature comfort.'

'Ah, well, that's because you are a young man,' Pollack said graciously. 'To the young the inner fire is so bright, so intense, that its warmth blots out everything. But when one becomes old, as I am, the blood runs thin, the inner fire sinks down, the skin is more sensitive, the bones frailer, the nerves closer to the surface, every tiny irritation becomes insufferable, every little frustration an exquisite torment.'

'Oscar Wilde,' Seymour Waxler said, clearing his throat, 'once said that it was a pity to waste youth on the young.'

'What have we here? A wit? A raconteur?' Pollack said with delight. 'You see, Julius, how deep Seymour's talent lies? Not merely a brilliant observer of the contemporary scene, with a genius for close-textured writing, but also a young man schooled in the classics. How many of our contemporary playwrights could quote Oscar Wilde? Could Paddy Chayefsky, for instance?'

Seymour Waxler remained silent, puffing importantly on his meerschaum.

Julius beamed on Waxler. Delighted that the young man should so please Pollack. It made him feel proud of himself for having found him.

'So many young writers these days,' Pollack went on, graciously accepting a light for his cigarette from one of Waxler's flaring kitchen matches, 'are incapable of the literary niceties. I don't ask them to write as Wilde and Molnar. Perhaps that is a mode now gone from the theatre. But if they could merely *appreciate*. If they could simply enjoy and understand the works of such men. How much it could give them in their artistic enrichment. Art does not spring from the sterile synthetic. It comes from the rich humus of the civilizations that have preceded us. In every word we speak to one another we echo the sounds of Chaucer's pilgrims, and those are, in a sense, the *modern* sounds. Think how much more ancient our tongue is. I am no linguist, no semanticist, but surely the roots of English lie in the Indian civilizations. And I find among so few young writers any appreciation for the continuity of their art, any understanding that they are products of the ages which went before them. In every character in your play, Seymour, I feel an awareness of the theatrical spirit. An awareness which reaches back to the mystery plays.'

'Mystery plays don't interest me,' Seymour Waxler said, clearing his throat again. 'I don't care much for Agatha Christie and all that stuff.'

'No, I was speaking of the earliest plays of the Greek theatre,' Pollack said, and then laughed and pushed against Waxler's beefy shoulder with his slender hand. 'Ah, you were pulling my leg!'

Waxler smiled vaguely and retreated behind his pipe, his little yellow-brown eyes narrowing to hide their confusion.

'Such a charming way of putting the old pedant in

his place,' Pollack said. 'I am too slow on my feet for you younger fellows. Such nimble minds, so agile in your movement from one thought to another. The speech of your play reflects that. The modern man's impatience with long-winded, laborious, overly full speeches. The quick staccato of response. The *mot juste* speared in mid-air as a fisherman might impale precisely the flying fish of his choice. Such éclat, such bravura!' Pollack tickled the air with his fingers to signify his exquisite frustration. In his pleasure he leaned forward and nipped Julius's cheek. 'My boy, I can't tell you how pleased I am with you for having found Seymour. A find! A genuine find in an otherwise barren theatrical season!'

Julius blushed, a little from the strength of Pollack's bony pinch.

'What do you think about the casting?' Seymour Waxler asked, clearing his throat.

Pollack threw up his hands. 'The impatience of modern youth. All business. All professionalism.' He beamed on Seymour Waxler. 'My dear boy, I have been complimenting you. I have been sitting here and articulating, in my crude way, my pleasure over your abilities. There was a time when an artist might graciously accept such compliments. But not today. Not the rough-and-ready craftsmen of our modern theatre. Fine speeches, fine feathers, they say! *Pouf* to all that! Let's to things which matter. To the heart, the kernel, the nut of the matter. A play is for players. And a play and players for a stage. And a stage, a play, and players are for an audience. What of that?' Pollack leaned forward intimately, placing his hand on his bony breast. 'If I say no more kind words about you, it is not because I have not the will nor the taste for them. But I am deferring to the heat which you, as an artist of the theatre, bring to me.'

Pollack was interrupted by a call to the phone.

'Perhaps it is Paris this time,' he said, rising. 'Excuse me. I won't be but a moment.' They followed his thin, awkward figure for a moment and then were thrust upon one another for company. Julius hesitated, watching the young genius, thrilled with Pollack's words. Waxler fixed his small yellow-brown eyes on the immutable middle distance of eternity and smoked.

'Tell me,' Julius asked, leaning forward in the friendliest fashion, 'what is your mother's maiden name?'

We, the undersigned, do protest and abhor the condition and nature of the theatrical district of the city of New York. Specifically that area from Forty-second Street on the south, to Fifty-fifth Street on the north, from the Avenue of the Americas (Sixth Avenue) on the east to Eighth Avenue on the west. We do protest that the American theatre should find itself cheek to jowl with cheap and noxious commercial enterprises, including ill-smelling food stores, noisy record shops, boardwalk gambling enterprises, bogus auctioneer palaces . . .

The petition ran on for two pages, a thousand of which lay in heaps beside the mimeograph machine. Julius's arm ached from cranking the handle.

All about the Leydecker living-room there were stacks of such forms. Her father, Mr. Leydecker, carefully stapled together healthy books of petitions. His daughter, with her Dutch-girl blonde haircut and fair eyes, neatly stacked the finished books.

They looked up when the whir and swish of the machine stopped.

'Are you tired, darling?' she asked Julius.

'Don't we have enough?' Julius asked.

'I want a million signatures,' her father said firmly.

Julius began to calculate in the dust on the machine with his finger. Twenty places for signatures remained at the bottom of each petition. To have a million . . . Julius's eyes bulged. Fifty thousand petitions! And the counter on the mimeograph machine only went to 9,999. Of course, oooo could mean 10,000. The counter now only stood at 1,632.

'May I rest?' Julius asked in a small voice.

Leydecker glanced at the paper left.

'You'll need more paper,' he said, and rose and went to get his leather coat and his leather workman's cap. Putting them on, he went out of the house.

She smiled at Julius and came and sat in his lap. His arm throbbed so badly that he could get no pleasure from her sweet weight.

'I thought we might go out and eat some Chinese food,' Julius said.

'How sweet,' she replied, and blew gently at his forelock.

'What's your first name?' Julius asked.

'Daphne,' she said with surprise. 'Didn't you know?'

'No,' he said. 'My mother spoke about you at dinner last week and wanted to know your first name and I realized I didn't know it. Daphne,' he said, testing the name. It had an odd, sweet, exotic quality.

'Is that all your mother wanted to know about me? My name?'

'No,' Julius said. 'She did want to know more. About your parents, what your father did and so on.'

'You know so much about me and I know so little about you,' she said softly. 'Tell me something.'

'There's nothing to tell. I am Julius Schapiro. I am twenty-four years old. I was born in New York City. I was graduated from Tilden High School in Brooklyn. I failed out of Brooklyn College at the end of my freshman year, and I work for Theodore Pollack Productions.'

'And you love me,' she said coquettishly. 'You forgot to add that.'

'And I love you,' he said, kissing the lobe of her ear.

'What other important things have happened to you

besides loving me?' Daphne asked, snuggling down more comfortably for a long recital.

'Well,' Julius said, and began to think. One by one he discarded memories. Not large enough. Not vivid enough. Not satisfying enough. 'Nothing,' he finally concluded.

'Oh, Julius!' she said, half with an air of disappointment and half with an air of relief. 'Is that all that's happened to you?'

'Yes,' Julius said soberly. 'But then, I'm not very old.'

'That's true,' she said, and traced her finger along his cheekbone. 'You are young. Nice and young.'

'What important things have happened to you?'

She straightened herself up importantly in his lap and recited. 'I am Daphne Leydecker. I am twenty years old. I was born in Babylon, Long Island. I went to primary school in Athens. Secondary school in Rome. I had private tutoring in Kobe and Geneva. I was a virgin until I was twelve years old. I was sold into slavery in Marrakech when I was sixteen and bought back when I was seventeen. I have been arrested eight times and have been in jail six times. I have been a member of the Communist party, the Anarcho-Syndicalists, the Monarchist party, the Falangist party, the Labour party, the Blue Dragon Society, and the Algerian Nationalist party. I smoked hashish for the first time when I was fifteen. Heroin when I was fourteen. I have killed three men and two women and have been shot twice, stabbed four times, and whipped three times.' She paused, and with a radiant smile added, 'And I am in love with a nice young man named Julius Schapiro.'

He looked at her with glazed eyes. 'You are lying,' he finally said hoarsely.

'No, I am not,' Daphne said, looking at him with mild surprise. 'Truth seekers never lie. Why should we?'

'All that's really happened to you?' Julius asked, horror-struck.

'Yes, of course,' she said. 'Is it very hard to believe?'

Julius shook his head weakly. 'How – how have you managed to live to be twenty?'

'I don't know. It hasn't been so hard.'

'Shot and stabbed.'

'Oh, mere flesh wounds,' Daphne said deprecatingly.

'Hashish and heroin,' Julius said feebly.

'Not much of either. Just for the sensation. The first tastes like vile tobacco and the other makes you feel good. But I don't feel depressed much, so I didn't use much of it. Anyway, it is terribly expensive,' she said with a sober air.

'In jail, too,' Julius said, staggered.

'Mostly for political activities and once it was a complete mistake. They thought I was someone else. They released me before nightfall.'

'How – how many men?' Julius asked, burning with shame.

'Oh, I've never kept count of that,' she said with a smile. 'Only of the times when I've been pleased. And they haven't been too many. Not really. You're the only one who's ever pleased me since Marrakech.'

'That was four years ago,' he said, horrified. What had he been doing four years ago? Taking chopped-egg sandwiches from home to his job at Pollack's office.

'Then it wasn't the man who owned me but one of his young servants. A sweet young man like you.'

'The man who owned you –' Julius said, feeling his heart recoiling.

'Oh, pooh! That foolish old man. He owned ten women, and his own wife had a moustache. Do you think he ever really had the energy for all of us? Think of all it takes from a man for just one woman. And can you imagine ten of us and his wife, as well? He just wanted to play the Moslem lover, that's all. Most of the time he just wanted to look at us. That's all he could do – look. And sometimes when he came to look we threw things at him and he ran away.'

'But you must have danced for him,' Julius said, remembering vividly an M-G-M picture about harem life. Of course, the censors couldn't pass the whole truth.

'Dance? I can't dance at all,' she said with surprise. 'You aren't jealous of that old fool, are you, my darling?' She touched his lips solicitously with her fingers.

'Your father!' Julius remembered in anger. 'Where was he all this time?'

'He was with me, when he wasn't in jail or on his job.'

'And he knew all this? And did nothing?' For instance, he didn't go insane or kill himself? Or anything at all like that?

'He bought me back from slavery,' she said. 'Although I would have gotten away anytime I felt like it. But I thought the political situation was bad for the moment and decided it would be safer under someone's protection.'

'But how could he be so – so – careless!' Julius cried out.

'But he did care!' Daphne said. 'He spent a lot of money to buy me back. That's the game the fat old fool played. He pretended to be terribly in love with me when the fact of the matter was that he didn't love me at all. I wasn't to his taste. Too thin. You should see what he preferred. A coal-black Sudanese with the largest behind I've ever seen. She did have lovely teeth and a sweet voice. I will say that for her. But stingy, definitely stingy.'

'And your mother!' Julius suddenly recalled.

'Oh, she was away most of the time. There was an

Italian she was mad about at the time. But he was arrested for something illegal, and she left him. She caught up with us in Lisbon before we came to New York.'

'And she had nothing to say about what had happened?'

'She was very angry with my father about some silver she gave him. He had sold it, I think. I don't recall now. I suppose it was to help buy me back.'

'And your mother objected?' Julius asked with a voice of rising indignation.

'Well, to be completely accurate, my father didn't use all of that money for me. It was solid silver, you know. A complete service for twenty. It had been a present from her mother, you know. Mother is a sentimental woman.'

Julius shook his head. No, no, he wouldn't believe it. That last thing about her mother being sentimental. It was too monstrous. Too incredible. He looked at her. So unspoiled. So perfect. So flawless. To have been a slave. A naked slave in an Arab's harem. To have smoked hashish. To have taken heroin. A member of secret parties. In jails. In the arms of God knew how many men. He searched the faded blue eyes, the fine skin of her face. Why hadn't such brutalizing left its mark on her? Where were the traces of such a depraved and debauched life?

'Swear to God that you are not lying!' Julius cried out in an agony.

'But why should I swear to a non-existent being?' Daphne asked.

'Tell me the truth,' Julius pleaded, tears starting in his eyes. 'I will believe you.'

'But that is the truth,' Daphne said. 'Did you want more details?'

'No, no,' Julius cried out, shuddering.

'Why, you are trembling.' Daphne said with wonder and pity. She kissed his cheek. 'And you feel so cold and moist. Are you well?'

He got up, and she stood beside him.

'I don't feel well,' Julius said, his arm numb now. 'I can't turn that machine any more. I can't produce fifty thousand copies.'

'Of course not,' Daphne said. 'You poor thing. Why don't you go and lie down in my bed? I'll join you later and comfort you.'

'No, no, I won't. I can't,' Julius said, suddenly frightened. 'I love you. How could I add to your degradation?'

'What degradation?' she asked politely, her candid blue eyes puzzled.

'Oh, you little child,' he said, and held her face between his hands, tenderly, lovingly.

She moved towards him, and he backed away from her at the hips.

'Julius,' she said in a small reproving way.

'I must not take advantage of you. It would be wrong,' he said. That made him feel stronger. Yes, that was it. It would be wrong. She had no sense of morality. He would be as wicked as that evil old Arab bastard if he touched her now. God, what monstrosities she had endured! How the human flesh could bear such humiliation! And such tender, almost childlike flesh! 'Tell your father,' he said, 'that I'll be back to help with the mimeographing. Sometime this week. I'm not sure.'

'Julius!' Daphne cried out, 'You will be back, won't you?'

'Oh, yes,' Julius said sturdily. 'I will never leave you to that – that monster!' He hurried out lest she try to kiss him. He hurried down the stairs. When he was in the vestibule, he heard her door open and she leaned over the banister and called down.

'What? What is it, my beloved?' he called back, his nerves tensing. Was she in some danger?

'What monster did you mean?' she called down.

'Your father!' he shouted back, feeling foolish, and hurried out before she could answer.

When he returned home, he was silent and grim. His mother, who had been watching television, came out and asked him if he would have some milk and cookies before retiring. He gave her a bittersweet smile. What did his innocent mother know of the world? Milk and cookies! How innocuous! How innocent! He shook his head and touched her face briefly, tenderly, mysteriously, and went off to his room to think, to brood.

He stared out at the silent night over the East Bronx. In the far-off distance, the elevated train moved with brilliant blue flashes beneath its wheels as the contact shoe jumped a break in the charged third rail. What a life! So young and yet so much had happened to her! Athens. A child in Athens with the classic purity of the Parthenon. The Greek light on her small face, the same childish eyes and the blonde Dutch-girl bob. And Rome. A serious schoolgirl with a black schoolgirl's uniform with black stockings, going to school. A school run by nuns, perhaps. Nuns with strange, swooping white headgear. A virgin until she was twelve. Who was her first despoiler and where did it happen? An innocent girl walking primly through the Trastevere, ignoring the filth and dirt. Some gang of Roman urchins? Had she been forced or had she been curious? Or had it happened with an older man? Some pervert from the Via Veneto. A fat Dutch lecher sitting on the chairs in front of Doney's. 'Kommt heer,' he said, holding up some bauble. Better not to think of the seduction in some hotel room. And Kobe. What was she doing in Japan? The *Blue* Dragon Society? He had heard of the Black Dragon Society. But that was composed of Japanese militarists. Who were the Blue Dragons? And what need had they of her blonde, blue-eyed innocence?

He gnawed his fingernails and stared out of the window. He could hear the laughter from the comedian's late night show on NBC.

He began to tremble. Now, now, he said to himself. None of that. We have to be reasonable. Yes, reasonable. All that's past. All of that is gone. This is the United States of America and everything is well cared for here. No slavery. No hashish. No heroin – except among Negroes, Puerto Ricans, and progressive-jazz musicians. No one to shoot, stab, or whip her here. No secret organizations for her to join. No need for her to be arrested or put into jail. She loves you. She won't be unfaithful. If her parents are bad influences, then he could free her. And anyway, how do you know all that is true?

Julius sat bolt upright in his chair, electrified. Let's be reasonable about this. Let's be hard-boiled. How did she do all that goddamned travelling? Athens, Rome, Marrakech, Kobe, Geneva, Lisbon, New York. Christ! That's almost completely around the world. Two abortions? Come now. Let's be a little more realistic. She was, as she said, born in Babylon. That makes her an American citizen. If she's twenty years old, that means she was born in 1939. Born in Babylon, New York. Nineteen thirty-nine was the beginning of the war in Europe. How did she get to Athens in the middle of the war to start her schooling? Right? Right! The Germans were in Greece in 1940. Did they allow American citizens to go to Greece just like that? With the Germans occupying? But wait a minute. Suppose she had gone to Greece when she was seven or eight. That would have been 1945 or 1946. Still tough to get to Europe. But not impossible. Oh, Christ, you're not going to believe all that hooey, Schapiro, are you? The *Blue* Dragon Society? Ah, come on now! Sold into slavery in Marrakech? An American citizen? A little sixteen-year-old blue-eyed blonde girl? With an American passport? Schapiro, you're being sold a barrel of baloney! Here's the true story: Born in Babylon, Long Island, in 1939. Educated – Babylon public schools. Moved to New York when she was teenager. Christ, she might have been at Tilden High School! How would you know? A freshman when you were struggling with the irregular verbs at Brooklyn College. Can't you see her mincing along Church Avenue in Brooklyn with those hideously swollen white athletic socks and her arms filled with books on civics, French, economic geography and history and English? Sure you can. A cute little chick, worried about her grades, but not about getting an escort for the Junior prom. Popular, too. Check the Tilden High School year-books. You'll find that sweet face smiling out at you in a rank of girls taking a commercial course. And the legend beneath her name? Junior Prom Committee, Spanish Office, Girls' Intramural Basketball. No slavery in Marrakech. No Blue Dragon Society. No hashish. No heroin. No abortions. You make up songs, don't you? She makes up stories. So what's wrong with a highly imaginative, sensitive young American girl? Your story was dull enough. She made up her mind that hers wouldn't be. That's it.

Julius got up from his chair with a smile and went into the living-room. 'Ma,' he asked, 'where are the cookies?'

There was a stiff spring breeze blowing on Sixth Avenue, and Julius had a hard time keeping the petitions from blowing away. He wished now that he had been able to set up a small card table and staple the petitions down. He had been at the corner for about a half hour without getting more than five signatures, and they were from a group of high-school kids. He would have to destroy that sheet because they were all jokers. One of them had signed Joe Stalin, another Adolf Hitler, and other such nonsensical names.

Twice the mounted police officer had walked his horse by, eyeing Julius and his petitions.

A prowl car came up and the police officer beckoned Julius over. 'What's the dodge, fella?' the officer asked.

'I'm trying to get this petition signed.' He handed over a copy to the officer, who read it slowly. The police officer handed it to his partner. Julius suddenly realized that he was the centre of interest for a small crowd. The small crowd grew to a larger crowd and in surprisingly few moments the crowd was blocking traffic. The mounted officer came up on the huge horse that took such small mincing steps.

'All right, move along, move along,' the mounted officer said to the crowd, and it began to move slowly, looking back.

'What's this all about, fella?' the officer behind the wheel asked.

'It's all right there in the petition, Officer,' Julius said, shaking slightly, the old fear of policemen affecting him. He had made up his mind not to be frightened. He wasn't doing anything wrong. The Bill of Rights gave every American the right to petition and redress.

'Yeah, I know, I know,' the policeman said. 'But what's it all about? You a member of the party?'

'No, sir. I am a Truth Seeker.' That, Julius realized, was a lie.

'What are those?' his partner asked, folding up the petition and putting it on a clip board.

'A group of people seeking the truth.'

'Now, come on, fella, be reasonable. You a religious organization?'

'Oh, no, sir,' Julius said. 'As a matter of fact, most of us don't believe in organized religion.'

'Political party?'

'No, sir. Most of us have nothing to do with politics,' Julius said.

'Come on, fella, we can't spend the whole night here. What the hell are you?'

'A Truth Seeker,' Julius said firmly. The police officer behind the wheel opened the door of the prowl car brusquely, hitting Julius in the genitals with the edge of the door. Julius bent over slightly, tears of pain springing into his eyes. The police officer was as tall as Julius but heavier, bulkier.

'Now, don't be a hard case,' the police officer said. 'I ask you a question and you answer it.' He looked up at the mounted officer. 'How long has he been here?'

'About an hour,' the mounted officer said. 'There's another one over on Seventh and one on Broadway and one on Eighth.'

'All like him?'

The mounted officer shook his head. 'An old guy with

a tough-looking beak. A big fat broad on Broadway and one of those punks with a beard on Eighth.'

'How many people you got around here?' the police officer asked Julius.

'There are eight of us.'

'Planning to do a little demonstration later on?' the police officer asked, hitching up his trousers.

'No, sir. Just collecting signatures.'

'You got any identification on you?'

'My name is Julius Schapiro.'

'Let's see your driver's licence.'

'I don't drive a car.'

'Draft registration.'

'I haven't got that. I was rejected two years ago.'

'You're supposed to carry that, buddy.'

'I don't see what for. There's no war on,' Julius said, wondering if the police officer was right.

The police officer leaned close to him and lowered his voice. 'Now don't give me any of your lip or I'll kick you in the balls right now.'

'You already have – with the edge of the door,' Julius said, angry.

'All right. Now, get off the street. Right now. I don't want to see you again tonight or any other time. If I do, I'll shag your tail in. Now, stick that junk inside your coat pocket and move.' The policeman's hard body shoved Julius aside as he whipped the door open. Julius avoided the edge of the door just by a hair's breadth. The prowl car pulled away and headed for Seventh Avenue. The mounted officer looked down from his Olympian perch.

'You heard him. Do what he says, kid. The detectives in this precinct are mean.'

Julius nodded his head. It seemed to him that the mounted officer was kind. Why was he kind and the prowl car officer such a Cossack? Had it something to do with his horse? Perhaps riding a horse gave a man dignity that sitting behind the motor of a cheap car did not. Julius rolled the petitions up and stuffed them into his coat pockets. His coat bulged away from him ludicrously as he walked over to Seventh Avenue to tell Mr Leydecker.

When he got to Seventh Avenue he saw a large mob gathered at the corner. He could make out the top of the police car. He had the feeling that there was going to be trouble. Mr Leydecker was not going to let anyone slam a door into his private parts. In a crack formed by the shifting of the crowd he saw Mr Leydecker's face close to the officer's face. Flint meeting steel. There had to be a spark. There was a commotion and now the crowd surged as the police officer moved Leydecker up towards the building. Another car came down the street.

The mounted officer brought his horse mincing along the street to Seventh Avenue.

A car stopped and two men in soft hats got out and took Julius by each arm. 'Police,' they muttered and pushed him into their unmarked car.

Julius sat between the two men in the back seat, surprised. He glanced back out of the window and saw the crowd being broken up by mounted officers. One of them had pointed him out to the detectives. And he had done what they had asked him to do. It was treachery.

They brought him to the police station and he sat in front of the detectives in shirt sleeves and answered the questions as to his name and age and address and employer's name and address.

Mr Leydecker soon appeared, his clothes rumpled, still clutching an armful of petitions. The secretary appeared in the company of two tough-looking policewomen, one with grey hair and a sallow complexion. They had also brought in the fat sighing man and the thin slat of a lady with a bun. But not the bearded young man and not Daphne.

They were all taken in a closed police van to night court and were then brought out in the company of drunks and vagabonds and common gamblers, who were the best dressed of them all.

There was an audience in the night court, and as each defendant stepped before the judge, there were lines and cues and laughter. The judge seemed to enjoy his role.

'This is the fourth time you've been here for drunk and disorderly behaviour, Patrick.'

'Yes, your honour,' the drunk said sadly with a faint brogue.

'I know every Irishman loves his whisky. But with you it seems to be a more serious matter, Patrick.'

'Oh, your honour, I can't help meself,' the drunk said, and there was laughter.

'Would you want me to help you, Patrick?'

'Oh, if your honour only could.'

'I could put you out of touch with whisky for a while.'

'Oh, your honour, that would be no help atall, atall.' Laughter.

'I think it would be an immense help. Ten dollars or ten days.'

'I have no money, your honour.'

'The city of New York has plenty, Patrick.'

The bailiff took the drunk by the arm, and there was a small outburst of laughter. The judicial wit turned over some papers, took a sip of water.

I'm under arrest, Julius suddenly thought with horror. I'm in court. I have a police record. They have my finger-prints. He looked at Mr Leydecker. Flint. At the secretary. Flint. At the lady thin as a slat. Flint. At the man with the sighs. Bemused amiability.

A prostitute stood before the judge.

'The police officer said you were soliciting.'

'Your honour, I said nothing to him. So help me. Why would I be talking to strange men in the street?'

'Did he speak to you first?'

'He didn't speak to me an' I didn't speak to him.'

'Did he look at you?'

'Well, my goodness, your honour, everyone looks. I mean, I'm not exactly repulsive, am I?'

'The court offers no opinion.'

Laughter.

'According to the police officer's report you are employed as a model.'

'That's right, your honour.'

'Are you working now?'

'Not right now. Just calls. Day to day.'

'Calls from whom?'

'From photographers, magazines, agencies. Things like that.'

'Which photographers, which magazines?'

'Oh, I can't think of them offhand, just like that. I've got them all written down in my appointment book.'

'And your appointment book is home?'

'Yes, your honour.'

'The models I know have always carried their appointment books with them.'

'Well, I don't get so many jobs I can't remember them in my head.'

'Oh, I see. You do remember them. But not the names of the people, the photographers, the magazines.'

'Well, for instance, I did some modelling for *Vogue*.'

'Ah, *Vogue*. My wife reads *Vogue*. I am sorry to say I do not. Do you do much modelling for *Vogue*?'

'Off and on.'

'How much off and how much on?'

Laughter, from the prostitute as well.

'I did not intend for you to construe the meaning you evidently have,' the judge said. 'How often do you model for *Vogue*? In the past year, for instance.'

'Ten, twelve times,' she said.

'And what is the address of *Vogue* magazine's New York office?'

'Well, gee, your honour –'

'You don't know?'

'Not offhand.'

'Is it on Madison, Park, Fifth, or Sixth Avenue?'

The girl remained silent.

'Perhaps Lexington or Third,' the judge suggested.

The girl remained silent.

'Yes, I see,' the judge said. 'You really don't know. Well, at least you didn't lie and force us to check the Manhattan directory. I'll be frank with you. I don't know, either. But then, I've never modelled for *Vogue*.'

Laughter.

'Fifty dollars or twenty days.'

'Can I get change of a hundred, your honour?'

'Not from me, you can't. I'm only a lower-municipal-court justice. Try the clerk.'

Laughter.

And now it was their turn. Julius stood beside the secretary. Leydecker stared ahead with solemn eyes. Brave, unafraid. Julius made up his mind that he would say nothing funny.

'Were you distributing these petitions?'

'No, your honour,' Leydecker said. 'Not distributing them. Asking for signatures.'

'Did the police officer ask you to desist?'

'He told me to desist,' Leydecker said firmly.

'You were creating a disturbance.'

'There was no disturbance until the police officers arrived. They created the disturbance.'

'Now, now,' the judge said with mild reproof in his voice. 'It is their job to protect the public.'

'We are part of the public,' Leydecker said.

'Were you being molested in any way?'

'By none but the police.'

'Don't trade verbal niceties with me, sir. By standing in one spot and importuning passers-by you were interrupting the flow of pedestrian traffic in a very busy thoroughfare. Perhaps one of the busiest thoroughfares in the world.'

'And when merchants importune passers-by with the loud and vulgar claims for their shoddy merchandise, do they not, also, interrupt the flow of pedestrian traffic? And on the busiest thoroughfare?' Leydecker asked bitterly.

'Are merchants doing that on Broadway these days?'

Laughter.

'By displays, by signs, by loud-speakers,' Leydecker replied.

'From premises which they own or rent,' the judge observed. 'You, however, appropriated public property for your enterprise. Without, I may add, the consent of the people of New York or their legally constituted authorities.'

'I was selling nothing. I was seeking to exercise a right possessed by more than merely the people of the City of New York. A right possessed by all of the people of the United States.'

'My, my,' the judge said. 'I did not realize we were dealing with such grand issues. I thought we were merely trying to discover what constituted a public nuisance.'

'The right of petition, I believe, is the right I am discussing,' Leydecker said haughtily.

'I suspected it was. You, however, misinterpret the
limits of the right of petition. It does not give you the
right to cause a public disturbance. Nor does it give you
the right to behave in a disorderly fashion.'

'I was not behaving in a disorderly fashion,' Julius
said, speaking up loudly.

The judge turned his eyes towards him. 'And what is
your name, son?'

'Julius Schapiro, your honour.'

'And were you distributing the petitions as well?'

'I was not. I was told to move along by a police
officer in a prowl car. He told me to put my petitions
away in my pockets. I did so. I put them away. Then I
walked towards Seventh Avenue, where I saw the crowd
about Mr Leydecker. While I was watching, two detectives came up to me, took me by my arms, and arrested
me.'

'Just like that? While you were innocently watching?'

'Yes, sir. While I was watching.'

'And how did the detectives know you had been distributing the petitions if you were so innocent?

'I was pointed out to them by a mounted trooper.'

'I knew the cavalry would arrive here someplace.'
Laughter.

'He had seen me warned by the police in the prowl
car on Sixth Avenue. He had also seen me put the petitions away in my coat pockets and he had watched me
walk away.'

'But you didn't walk away, did you?'

'But I did.'

'No. You could have walked away by walking east or
even north or even south. You walked the only direction
in which you could have caused an additional disturbance.

You walked west – to your confederates. That's why you were pointed out and arrested.'

There was a sprinkle of applause. Such wit. Such acumen. Such powers of deduction!

Julius wanted to protest but he could not help but admire the judge's brilliance. It was neatly put. Of course, he had no intention of causing a disturbance. But how did the officers know that? They could only read his intentions by his behaviour.

'Now, I won't go into each of the cases individually. I am aware that –'

'Have you read the petition?' Leydecker asked brusquely.

'You must not interrupt, sir,' the judge said gently.

'Have you?' Leydecker persisted.

'Why? Are you soliciting my signature now?'

Laughter.

'How can you presume to judge something you don't understand?' Leydecker asked.

'My dear man, I judge because the City of New York pays me my salary to do so.'

'I did not ask why you judge, I asked how,' Leydecker nagged.

'Don't be witty, sir,' the judge said. 'Wit in this court can cost you money.'

'Why won't you read the petition?' Leydecker asked.

'Because the content of the petition has nothing to do with the charges against you.'

'Read the petition,' Leydecker said stubbornly.

Julius began to feel uncomfortable. Why was Leydecker being so stubborn? What difference did the petition make?

'I warn you sir,' the judge said gaily, 'the content of the petition may only make your position worse.'

Laughter.

Julius smiled. It was neatly put. He felt irritation when Leydecker spoke.

'I want the petition read by the court,' Leydecker said.

'Aloud?'

Laughter.

'Know what you are judging,' Leydecker insisted.

'Now that will be quite enough. You are verging on contempt. Insouciance I like. Sauciness gets by. Impudence is the limit I will tolerate and then only when it comes from likelier-looking creatures than yourself. You have gone beyond impudence and are tramping near the court's toes. Beware.'

The felicity of speech so enchanted the night-court audience that it applauded. No sprinkle. An honest pattering. Julius almost joined in the applause. Leydecker, that ape, deserved it.

'I don't want to be harsh with you. You are evidently all decent people – if somewhat bemused by something. If it matters, sir, I have read the petition, and if you had approached me in an orderly and discreet manner to sign that petition, I would have cheerfully put my name to those sentiments. But you must understand that the City of New York is a vast complex, supporting a population in excess of eight million people. The simplest process in the management of the city is enormously complicated by such great numbers. No one wishes to infringe upon the rights of any citizen – I least of all. Certainly the police of New York, one of the finest forces of uniformed men in the world, are capable of using good judgement. They would not have brought you here if you had not compelled them to do so. The last thing a policeman wants to do is to arrest someone. It takes up too much of his time. The last thing I want to do is to sentence people to prison. It eats up too much of the tax revenues. And yet here you are and here I am and you all face fines and imprisonment. Why? Because you have interrupted the processes of the city. If we tolerated too many interruptions of the processes, life would become chaotic. Traffic could come to a standstill. From snarled traffic to snarled transportation generally is just a step. From blocked transportation to crises is just another step. From crisis to crisis the matters would grow worse. Actual want, medical and fire emergencies would occur without any chance of relief. People would die. Others would panic and the city could become a nightmare for all of us. All because of you and your petitions? No. Not just you. But you and other people and still other people. Everyone has grievances, ladies and gentlemen, every society worth its salt allows those grievances to be aired. But not at the cost of municipal good order. I therefore find you each guilty of creating a disturbance, fine you each ten dollars or ten days in prison. I also suspend each of your sentences.'

This time the applause was solid. Not pattering. But solid third-act applause, and Julius proudly joined it, beating his hands together. This was a performance worthy of applause. Intelligent, humane, broad-minded, warm and yet firm, judicial.

You are verging on contempt. Insouciance I like. Sauciness gets by. Impudence is the limit I will tolerate and then only when it comes from likelier-looking creatures than yourself. You have gone beyond impudence and are tramping near the court's toes. Beware. Thus spoke Manhattan Night Court's star performer, balding, liver-spotted, blue-eyed, fifty-six-year-old Justice Thomas B. (for Boetia, rhymes with Police-yeh) Garrigan to a vocal group of disturbers of the peace who called themselves the 'Truth Seekers'. Seeking truth with a petition that called for the abolition of Broadway's honky-tonk midway, the truth seekers tangled traffic, tried the patience of New York's finest, found themselves haled before Justice Garrigan. He treated them with the grave courtesy and Irish wit that have made him the most quotable New York justice in recent history. Tammany's tiger, ears long perked to the brilliant patter of Justice Garrigan, thought it had found itself another likely candidate. Wit in an Irish judge in New York is as good as money in the bank. Tammany's tiger purred and put out, hopefully, a dish of political cream. One Truth Seeker (sentence suspended) summed up Garrigan's charm. Twenty-four-year-old truth-seeking playwright Julius Schapiro said, after he had joined in a spontaneous burst of applause over the jurist's eloquence: 'He told us more about the truth in his warning to us than I have ever found in my whole life. God bless him.' Tammany counted Schapiro's vote as a sure one.

'I said nothing of the kind,' Julius said to Evelyn as they looked at the magazine together.

'There you are, coast to coast,' Evelyn remarked. 'Why did you tell them you were a playwright?'

'I didn't,' Julius protested. 'I told him I worked for Mr Pollack. He didn't even know the name. They got everything mixed up.'

'Well, never mind. You got your name in twice,' Evelyn said soothingly, putting the magazine aside.

'I felt like such a fool,' Julius said.

'About being arrested?'

'About everything. Damned-fool petition. I don't know what they're hollering about. I like Broadway the way it is.'

'You would,' Evelyn said dryly.

'I never would have done it if it hadn't been for Daphne,' Julius said.

'No, you're kidding,' Evelyn said with a smile. 'Is that really her name?'

'Daphne Leydecker. It was her father's idea.'

'I didn't think a name like that would be her mother's.'

'No, I mean, about the petition. I nearly ruined my arm with that mimeograph machine.'

'Well, never mind, Julius. You're famous now. Now you'll be able to find a wife. You've got the sheen on you. Too bad they didn't run a picture of you.'

Pollack entered. 'Good morning, good morning.'

'Seymour Waxler called,' Julius said.

'Not now, not now,' Pollack said airily.

'Julius is famous,' Evelyn said with a grin, and flipped open the magazine. Pollack hung up his Homburg and chesterfield and put aside his cane. He took the magazine and walked slowly into his office, reading.

'I wish you hadn't shown him that,' Julius said unhappily.

Pollack appeared at his door in a short while, the magazine in his hand. 'Come in, my boy. Come in.'

Julius entered almost reluctantly. Pollack moved to the window overlooking the street and solemnly closed his fly.

'Julius, I am disappointed in you,' Pollack said, sitting down and shaking his head sadly.

'Really, Mr Pollack, it wasn't my fault –'

'You were arrested, weren't you?'

'Yes, but not through anything I had done.'

'If you were in trouble – why didn't you call me? Don't you know that I am available, day or night, at any hour to help my associates?'

Julius's heart softened. 'I didn't think.'

'It's obvious you didn't think, and that surprises me. For I had always thought you were a thoughtful person. And you are. You are. The mere fact that you braved arrest and imprisonment to protest over the shoddiness of Broadway is proof to me that you are a deeply thoughtful young man. I would expect you to do such a thing. But why did you forget me? Didn't you think that I, too, would feel as strongly as you?'

'Mr Leydecker wanted us to go out in the street to get signatures.'

'But of course he did,' Pollack paused. 'Who is Mr Leydecker?'

'He's the chairman of the Truth Seekers.'

'Ah, I see. And if you needed recruits for such a mission – why didn't you call on me?'

'But we were arrested!' Julius cried out.

Pollack smiled. 'And wasn't Galileo arrested? And wasn't Socrates arrested? And wasn't Jesus arrested? Think of all the noble minds and great hearts which have languished in prisons and tell me that to be arrested is not a badge of honour, a *cachet* of pride? I think how proud I would have been to stand before the bar of justice with you. Shoulder to shoulder.'

'But the judge made me feel that I was wrong.'

'Ah, Justice Garrigan. That cheap little night-court wit. What does he do? He sits up there on his lofty perch, his black robe hiding his gravy-stained clothing, and showers you with his so-called wit. How heroic of him! How grand, how noble! How did you play the scene, Julius?'

'I didn't play it at all.'

'Merely a theatrical figure of speech, of course. But how did you respond? How did you counter his feeble Hibernian humour?'

'As a matter of fact, he said very little to me. Mr Leydecker did most of the talking.'

'And Mr Leydecker?'

'They argued about what constituted a public disturbance.'

Pollack made small noises of distress. 'Badly managed, badly done. No riposte. No contest.' He tapped the magazine. 'They would not have been so abubble with Justice Garrigan's wit if I had been there.'

'He was clever,' Julius said.

'Clever? At whose expense? At the expense of drunks whose minds even when they weren't sodden with drink were dull and thick? Clever in parrying the brutish replies of gamblers whose only verbal facility has to do with the matter of mathematical odds? Conquering the debilitated back chat of sidewalk vendors? Is that clever? Was he crushingly successful in mocking prostitutes? You see, Julius, in night court, the offal of civilization drifts through. A moderately literate man can become a Solomon, a Psalmist, a Voltaire when he deals with such trash. How often does he have to cross swords with something sharper than lead pipe? Then, of course, you must reckon that he holds an exalted position. He is the judge and all who appear before him are minor felons. Not major felons, whose crimes might give him some reason for awe. No. Sidewalk spitters, subway smokers, pedlars without licences.'

Julius nodded his head thoughtfully. Mr Pollack was right. He had not considered Justice Garrigan in just that light. 'You certainly would have made him look sick,' Julius said loyally.

'I have no false modesty, my boy,' Pollack said. 'I would have made him look sick indeed. You understand how these magazine pieces are originated, don't you? They are almost always inspired by the subjects themselves through paid agents.'

'Always?' Julius asked, shocked.

'Always,' Pollack said flatly. 'You don't imagine that newspapers and magazines have the staff to screen the world, do you? To be everywhere to hear the *mot juste*, the perfect quip, to meet the colourful character? No, my dear boy. These things are fed to them by a tireless, imaginative paid army of press agents. They would be helpless without these men. Somewhere in the democratic machinery of our city there is a paid publicist whose clients are interested in Justice Garrigan. He whispers to a reporter outrageous legends concerning Garrigan's great wit, suggests an angle for his story. The reporter writes a small feature article on Garrigan and it is fed by his parent organization to subscribing newspapers. Nothing comes of it. The publicist urges the press-association reporter of local news to pay special attention to Garrigan's court, to collect *bon mots* and sparkling examples of repartee. These are fed to the magazine writer. Finally whipped out of his lethargy, he speaks to his sub-editor, who asks for a piece. A piece is written. It has no topical value. Garrigan will be on the night-court bench for years, perhaps. It is put aside. Garrigan can wait. One week a small hole appears in the make-up of the magazine. Enough room for an item. What of that judge in night court? They "punch" it up with some topical reference, trim it to a third of its original size, add a little "inside gossip" to make it appear more important, and there it is one bright morning for six million people to read, packaged as though it were a piece of fresh red meat lately cut from the body politic. When actually it is a bit of frozen carcass, nine, ten months old, defrosted in time for this edition.' Pollack shook his head. 'My boy, George Jean Nathan once remarked that enough publicity was attendant upon the production of each new theatrical enterprise to give the disinterested reader the impression that the play was equivalent to the Second Coming. I submit, however, that no theatrical publicity can ever compare to the publicity attendant upon the emergence of the new politician. He is given space free, for whatever he chooses to do or say. However inane, however vicious, however self-seeking, however patently false his behaviour and words, he is fully, generously reported. When you have an opportunity to share in his free public bath, cling to him for dear life, draw every precious drop for yourself that you can.'

'But I wasn't interested in publicity,' Julius said.

'Then you are not truly of the theatre,' Pollack said. 'Publicity is derived from the noun "public". It is the public which matters in the theatre. Not the actors, nor the writers, nor the directors, nor the theatre owners, and least of all the producers. It is the public. They will be served. They will be entertained. They will be diverted. The theatre is nothing without an audience. And to gain that audience, the theatre must be vibrantly, throbbingly alive to the problems of snaring public attention. You had an opportunity. You fumbled it. Not badly, I must admit. But you did not make the most of it. If I had been there in court with you, the article on Garrigan would not have been the article on Garrigan, but on Theodore Pollack.'

'Perhaps you'd like to go out with the Truth Seekers the next time ?' Julius suggested.

Pollack shook his head. 'Gone, gone, my boy. That opportunity is gone. No other story on Garrigan's night court will be carried for another year. No. I have undertaken this lecture for your future behaviour. When the opportunity presents itself, do not shrink from the limelight. Speak up. Clearly, sprightly, quotably. Never mind the sense. Be outrageous. Remember the motto of the theatre: Don't write, telegraph. Incidentally, it was a brilliant inspiration for you to have described yourself as a playwright.'

'I didn't,' Julius said. 'I told them play reader.'

Pollack shook his head sadly. 'You were saved from your own foolishness. What does play reader mean to the magazine's subscriber ? That is no characterization at all. Playwright is better. It has clearly defined limits. It stands out in print. Play reader is meaningless, garbled, confused. It distracts the mind which is trying to manage its feeding, a recollection of the day's appointments, and the news already read. In the vast complexity of the modern world there is no time for precise description. We are launched for the stars. Are we to stop for some little pup to tell us that he is a play reader and not a playwright ? What the devil do we know about plays ? Or even care ? It is enough for us to know that plays are written and not chisselled in stone, or cast in bronze, or stitched with thread. Plays are written. They are written by playwrights. Enough of plays. Who cares about the whole tiresome business of people who read plays for people who produce plays? That is all part of the lower intestine's fourth inner fold.' Pollack paused and looked at Julius carefully. 'And they are right. Why are they right? Because they are the public. Do you understand, my boy?'

'Yes, sir,' Julius said, dazzled.

'Then back to your work,' Pollack said. Julius rose and left. Pollack sighed and stretched himself out on his leather couch and went to sleep, exhausted by his labours.

One Truth Seeker (sentence suspended) summed up Garrigan's charm. Twenty-four-year-old truth-seeking playwright Julius Schapiro said ...'

That portion of the news clipping was circled in red and contained in a special folder which bore the special inked stamping 'HKS 120477 PS-LM-NC-224578R.' Some part of the stamped classification meant something to the governmental clerk in the Secret Service branch of the Treasury Department. Some of it meant something to her departmental chief. Some of it meant something to the IBM machine used by the Treasury Department's branch, the Secret Service. Some of it meant something to the archivist of the federal government. Some of it meant something to the auditing division of the Treasury Department and some of it meant something to someone whom no one really knew. And some of it meant nothing and someone knew that. And still some of it meant nothing and that was something no one knew. The last was something most closely guarded. The ignorance of the all-powerful always being the most closely guarded secret of Heaven. So it was on earth.

'Dear J. Edgar Hoover,' the letter in the file began. That mistaken beginning took six weeks in correction. The textual experts at the Federal Bureau of Investigation finally determined that the letter concerned an organization that threatened the elected officials of the United States. The nice point that had to be resolved was whether the elected officials were in executive or legislative branches of the federal government. If executive then they belonged to the FBI. However, the highest executive post was that of the chief executive of the United States, and the experts reasoned that the organization involved appeared to be threatening his life. That meant that the letter should properly be directed to the Secret Service, whose function it was, among other things, to safeguard the life of the political incumbent. The threats to the motion-picture industry, it was agreed, by a joint committee of textual experts from the FBI and the Secret Service, could safely be given over to the police department of the City of Los Angeles, California. The threats to the Jews, everyone agreed, were irrelevant and under no one's jurisdiction and so not susceptible of action, preventive or punitive. It was felt that it could safely be covered by local statutes concerning disorderly conduct.

'... *these communist reds* ...' the letter stated at one point. This, too, was submitted to textual analysis, and it was commonly agreed that the organization was not one of the front organizations associated with the Communist party of the United States. A check was made with undercover agents within the Communist party to discover if there had been, lately, any creation of an organization named the 'Truth Seekers'. The latest tele-typed reports from New York, Seattle, Detroit, Chicago, Los Angeles, St Louis, Hawaii, and Mexico City confirmed that no such organization had come into existence to the agents' knowledge. The specialist in fascist organizations was telephoned at his home in Arizona and asked if he had heard of the 'Truth Seekers'. Textual analysts had to wait until the specialist returned from an antique sale he had auctioneered before they had their answer. No. No such new organization. That exhausted the two major political divisions. Cranks were left. Then began a tedious survey of each city in the United States to determine what new crank organizations had been formed. Teletype messages from the greater Los Angeles area were still coming in volume when New York City reported that the organization was known there. One textual analyst discovered a copy of the national magazine in the men's washroom, and his eye was struck by the name in the news item on Justice Garrigan. It was brought to the attention of the Secret Service analysts.

'... *they are sending dangerous things through the mail* ...' the letter stated. A careful check was made with the postal authorities. The Truth Seekers did have an address, listed in care of Ernest Leydecker. A mail cover was taken. Each letter received or sent by the addressee was noted. Aside from the usual mail concerning sales, electric bills, magazine and record offers, book offers, concrete-subscription offers, accident- and health-offers, new-car offers, special travel offers, commercial-cleanser offers, burial-plot offers, stock-market-investment offers, music-instruction offers, hotel-vacation offers, concert-subscription offers, accident- and health-insurance offers, fire- and theft-insurance offers, mortgage-insurance offers, home-sale offers, home-purchase offers, home-fuel-oil offers, retirement-to-Florida offers, retirement-to-Long-Island offers, retirement-to-California offers, trailer-home offers, the mail was non-existent. The outgoing mail, on the other hand, was voluminous. It was recorded, by the postal authorities, that in the past month letters had been sent by the Truth Seekers to: the governors of the states of New York, California, New Jersey, Ohio, Iowa, Illinois, Kansas, New Hampshire, Vermont, Maine, Connecticut, and thirty other states; to the President of the United States, the Secretary-General of the United Nations, to the chairman of UNESCO, to the officers of the International Ladies

Garment Workers Union, to the officers of the Loew's corporation, to the officers of the Twentieth Century-Fox Film Corporation, to the officers of the Columbia Broadcasting System, to the officers of the National Broadcasting System, to the officers of the American Broadcasting System, to the officers of the Mutual Broadcasting System, to the Licence Commissioner of the City of New York, to the Police Commissioner of the City of New York, to the Mayor of the City of New York, to the chairman of the New York City Convention and Visitors' Bureau, to the chairman of the Forty-second Street Association, to the president of the American Bar Association, to the presiding justice of the Supreme Court of the State of New York, and to a further list of forty other, less-important, public figures. All mail, it was noted, was sent first class. No mottoes or slogans or printed matter appeared on the envelopes, and the postal authorities were satisfied that the letters contained nothing inflammatory, explosive, corrosive, or abrasive in its intrinsic nature. The envelopes were clean, white, of standard 10c. size, medium weight, fully sealed, correctly addressed, bearing proper postage as to weight limits and duly certified engraved postage stamps of the United States of America. In short, nothing to report.

The letter that had prompted the creation of the file was signed 'An American Citizen of Great Loyalty.' Analysts reported that the letter was mis-spelled in fourteen places, misaddressed on its envelope, mailed at the Bathgate Avenue Postal Station in the Bronx, New York, bore an improper amount of postage, and was written with a steel pen and blue waterproof ink.

The file, now sealed with wax seals, was sent as part of a courier's bag to New York from Washington and turned over to the chief of the Secret Service branch in New York City. He broke the seals, scanned the matter contained, buzzed for an agent, and turned the file over to him.

The agent, whose name was Hanrahan, sat down in his office, emptied the file, counted the number of exhibits. They ran to sixty, stacked them on his desk, and began to read. Eight hours later he closed the file with a sigh, counted the exhibits to satisfy himself that he had returned sixty of them, scooped together the thirty pages of notes he had made, and weighed them in his hand.

His superior looked in on him before leaving for the day.

'Well?' his superior asked.

'I'll look over my notes tonight and get to work on it in the morning,' Hanrahan said.

'Lock up the file,' his superior said, and waved his hat good night.

Hanrahan nodded his head foggily. He rose, walked to the security file, placed the file folder inside, and then locked the security file. He returned to his office, opened his brief case, and put the notes inside. He locked his brief case, put on his jacket, straightened his tie, and put on his hat and coat. Brief case in hand, he cast one last look at his office, snapped off the light, and closed the door.

Within ten minutes, the subway had taken him to the Battery. There he took the ferry to Staten Island, and watched, as he did every night, the lights of Manhattan.

An hour after supper he dried his last dish and went into the living-room. His mother had already turned on the television set and was crocheting as she watched.

He glanced at the show and watched secret agents wrestling with a lissom, buxom brunette in a too-tight dress slit to the middle part of her thigh. He went to get his brief case. Shots rang out from the speaker of the television set.

He returned to the living-room and dropped the brief case on the table. He moved the lamp aside and then examined the blunted ends of the pencils. He rose wearily with the pencils and went into the kitchen, where he opened the door to the food closet. The pencil sharpener was screwed to the back of the door. He carefully sharpened each of six pencils and blew the excess shavings from their points. He was about to close the door when his eye caught the apples. He took two of them and went to the sink and washed them. He re-entered the living-room and looked at the television screen. The brunette was tied to a chair, the ropes working into her heaving flesh as she cried out, 'Tonee, don't, don't tell them anyzing! Tonnee!' He dropped one apple into his mother's lap. She put down her crocheting and took up the apple and bit into it, her eyes fixed on the television screen. He returned to the table, still looking at the screen. He finally put his apple down and the pencils beside it. He opened his brief case and took out his notes. He bit into his apple and read as he took up a pencil and began to make notes.

Two hours later he had reduced the thirty pages of notes to ten.

'You going to be finished soon?' his mother asked without glancing away from the television set.

'Pretty soon, Mother,' he said, and looked through the ten pages. He added one final observation at the bottom of the tenth page. 'Shit,' he wrote, and underlined it.

You see it, Julie? Don't you? I mean, the sweep, the scope, hunh?' the man asked, excited.

'Oh, yes,' Julius replied, not certain that he did. But flattered, deeply flattered.

'We got to do something about the title,' the man's thin, dyspeptic-looking partner said in an appropriately sallow voice. 'I mean, Al, *The Truth Seekers* – Christ, it sounds like a religious show.'

'And what's wrong with that, hunh?' Al challenged his partner. 'Christ, the biggest sales in books – Norman Vincent Peale, Lloyd Douglas, Rabbi Liebman. The biggest movie money-makers – de Mille's stuff. Ever read the figures on church attendance? Up every year since the war. Religion's hit everything but television. And wait until we show the pilot. Christ, the networks'll cream in their pants. I tell you they're hot for it. Wide open. Just laying back and panting for it. And brother, we've got the property to ram it home and lock it in. They'll scream!'

'Did you ever write a screenplay for television?' the sallow partner asked Julius.

'Well –' Julius began hesitantly.

'Oh, hell, that's a detail!' Al said, brushing it aside with a sweep of his heavy arm. 'I've got two of the hottest TV writers in the business clawing each other's guts out to do the job. Actually, you won't have to lift a finger to write, Julie.'

'Oh, I see,' Julius said, not certain what Al meant.

'You can be script supervisor,' the sallow partner suggested.

'Associate producer!' Al said quickly. 'We'll get some bright little girl to handle script details. And that's all they'll be, believe me, mere details. What we want from you, Julie, is an assurance that the show will have integrity. Real integrity.'

'Well, I'm sure we all want it to have that,' Julius said soberly.

'Jesus!' Al said with an excitement that shook his enormous frame. 'I've been shaking ever since I spotted the item in the magazine. Ask Lou if that isn't so! Isn't it so, Lou?'

Lou nodded soberly. 'He's been hot as a two-dollar pistol ever since he saw it.'

'It hit me like a tidal wave,' Al said. 'The Truth Seekers! Not just of today, but of yesterday, of tomorrow. Those lonely, solitary great *great* figures who were seeking the truth. King Solomon, Caesar, Alexander the Great, Napoleon, Moses, the first man on the moon – that's for the truth seeker of tomorrow. Shaking, believe me. I was like a wild man. Ask Lou. Wasn't I like a wild man, Lou?'

'Like a wild man,' Lou confirmed, nodding.

'What an idea, I yelled! What a beautiful idea!' Al cried out, knotting up two immense fists and shaking them in the air. 'Think of it! Holy men, little men, little women, sinners, saints, kings, conquerors, generals, dictators – obsessed with one great stinking obsession! To seek the truth! To find the truth! Christ, I nearly went out of my mind. Didn't I, Lou?'

'Nearly out of his mind,' Lou said, nodding.

'I got to find this guy Julius Schapiro, I yelled,' Al said, his face contorted with pain. 'Lou, Lou, I yelled we've got to find this guy! We've got to find him! I called the magazine! I called the Writers Guild! I called the papers! I called the Dramatists Guild! I called the Coast! I called all the networks! I called every agent in New York. I must've made a hundred calls. Right, Lou?'

'He spent nearly two days on the telephone,' Lou said, shaking his head in awe.

'Julie,' Al suddenly said with savage intimacy, gripping Julius's forearm in an iron grip, 'there are cheap little bastards around this town who would have kept their mouths shut. They would have run up a quickie pilot with a cheap writer and peddled the series without calling you at all. Then, when they sold it, you'd have to whistle for your share of the receipts. Am I right, Lou?'

'Lots of grifters in the business,' Lou said sadly. 'We could tell you stories –' He trailed off unhappily, shaking his head and making a face filled with sallow grief.

'But I'm not like that. Neither is Lou. If God ever taught me anything, it was honesty, integrity. Lou and I are, I'm proud to say, almost the only honest independent TV-film producers on the East Coast. Maybe both Coasts.'

'Both Coasts, both Coasts,' Lou said, shaking his head vigorously.

'And it hasn't been easy, baby,' Al said. 'We've lost thousands, hundreds of thousands of dollars. Right, Lou?'

'I don't even want to think about it,' Lou said, flipping his hands sadly as he waved farewell to steamer trunks filled with money.

'Honesty has cost us a lot, Julie,' Al said with a sudden, deep intense sadness. 'But I can't help the way I'm made. I can't help it!' He squeezed Julius's forearm with such strength that Julius had a hard time suppressing the gasp of pain that came to his lips. 'Let them write what they will in the Great Big Book in the hereafter about

Lou Cohen and Al Douglas. But they will never write of us: "They f—— their fellow man." ' Al released Julius's arm and looked at Julius with eyes burning with emotion. 'Never,' he said hoarsely, reverently. 'In the Big Book up there,' he said, pointing a finger towards the ceiling of the restaurant, 'they won't say that about me or my partner. I'd like to see what they've written in the Big Book about other independent TV-film producers,' Al said with a voice husky with meaningfulness.

'Oh, boy, I can imagine,' Lou Cohen said with melancholy joy.

'Julie,' Al said with sudden, swift intimacy, dropping his voice and leaning closer. 'You're a Jewish kid, aren't you?'

Julius nodded silently, his eyes fixed on Al Douglas's heavy, intense face.

'We've spent only a half hour together but I love you as though you were my own flesh and blood. I'm Jewish, too. Douglas is a phony name. I didn't want to do it. I had to. In this business you deal with a lot of weird sorts. Believe me. Right, Lou?'

'Incredible!' Lou said, shaking his head.

'There are advertising agencies in this town that won't let Lou Cohen past the receptionist. Those lousy anti-Semitic bastards!' Al Douglas turned his face and spat on the restaurant floor. 'That's what I think of them! I deal with them. I drink their liquor, I talk their language, I get them broads, but I hate their guts. I laugh at their jokes. Even the Abie and Beckie ones, and, brother, it puts a knife in my guts. My father's name was Abraham. You know how I feel. Sometimes I feel as though I can't take it. I feel as though I'm going to take one of those cruds and throw him out of the window of his office.'

'He's got a terrible temper,' Lou said with awe.

'I don't, thank God. I never want to kill another man,' Al said. 'I can do it with my bare hands, believe me. God gave me a strong body and a pair of hands. But I don't kill anyone. I go out and slug my kidneys with double Scotches until I don't feel any more. All because I want to kill someone and I can't! So I get nothing out of the work I do. Nothing! But maybe two things. I like to help one of my own kind along. And I've got my pride in my integrity. When you shake my hand you need nothing else. Lou and I have been partners for nearly eighteen years and we've never had a written agreement. Am I right, Lou?'

'Not a scrap of paper between us,' Lou said.

'I've handled thousands of dollars, hundreds of thousands of dollars, and Lou has never asked me to account for a penny. Lou has handled as much, and I've never asked him. Because Lou knows that I wouldn't cheat him of the smallest penny and he wouldn't cheat me. My God, if I didn't have that, I'd have nothing! I'd go out and kill myself right now! Am I right, Julie?'

'You certainly are,' Julius said, awed and a little frightened by the massive Al Douglas.

'What the hell, we're all brothers here, aren't we?' Al asked, holding out a meaty palm. 'I could play it cosy and slip you a sheet of paper with a lot of legal garbage that would tie you up six ways from the middle. But I don't do business that way. Not with people of my blood, my race. Not with decent Jewish kids like yourself. I give you only my hand, and in that hand is Al Douglas and everything he's stood for all of his life. And when you take my hand, Julie, I want the same from you. I want to know that you feel the same about an agreement, a bargain. If you feel the slightest hesitation about it – if you don't believe every word I've told you about the kind of man I am – don't take my hand. Get up from this table and walk out of this goddamned restaurant and never come back. Don't, I beg of you, take my hand if you don't deep down in your guts believe that I'm a man you can trust. And don't give me your hand if you're the sort of guy I can't trust. If you have any intention, any idea in the back of your head that you will try to screw me later on – I beg you, don't take my hand. I'd rather lose my arm than have to throw this series out but I'd rather be dead than give my hand in trust to someone I can't trust. When you take my hand I accept you as a brother. Just remember that, Julie.'

Al Douglas put out his enormous hand, his eyes fixed on Julius. Julius felt his heart hammering with apprehension and excitement. He had never shaken hands under such a terrible obligation. Hypnotized, perspiring, he put out his hand, and it disappeared in an enormous clutch of meat. Al Douglas's features split into a smile, and Julius felt Al's heavy arm encircle his shoulders.

'Atta baby,' Douglas said lovingly. 'We're partners.'

Julius grinned and then shook Lou Cohen's moist bony fingers with a hearty rattle. Lou Cohen smiled a yellow smile.

'Partners!' Al said, and draped arms over both men.

When Julius left the restaurant it was with a deep feeling that he suddenly had great friends. And yet they were more than friends. They were his partners. He felt guilty that he had not explained that he was not a playwright, but Al himself had said that he would not have to do any writing. That would be handled by professional TV writers. All he had to do was to supply integrity, and he felt competent to do that. He wondered if perhaps they could work music into the shows. Perhaps some original songs. What a break! He wasn't quite clear as to what Al had in mind for the format of the show. It would come clearer in the succeeding weeks, when the script was written. But an opening song for the Truth Seekers. Seekers, seekers, seekers of the word. The word, the word, the word of truth, truth, truth, truth is the word. No, that wasn't too good. Too circular. Out of the ages, torn from the pages, the mysteries of the sages, the passions and the rages, we are the seekers, the speechless speakers, the seekers, the speakers, the seekers, of the word, the word, the word of truth. Hey, not bad.

> 'Out of the ages,
> Torn from the pages,
> The mysteries of the sages,
> The passions and the rages,
> We are the seekers,
> The speechless speakers,
> The seekers,
> The speakers,
> The seekers of the –
> Word.
> The word, the word,
> The word of truth!'

He read the lines half aloud to himself, seeking the beat, the rhythm of the words. It would have to be something scored heavily for rhythm. Something with drums. Something that started low and rose higher and higher in intensity. He saw in his mind's eye, a level plain with men marching across it. Tiny figures at first, then larger and larger, men with different costumes of all times, chanting, singing as they came, 'We are the seekers, the speechless speakers, the seekers, the speakers –'; their figures would come closer as the music swelled, and now the camera would see the object of their steady march across the level plain, mountain peaks, made holy with snow, pure in their intense coldness and in a circle about the highest peak, as though a halo, as the music rose higher and louder and more insistent and the tramping of feet stronger, a circle reading in white letters, 'A Codougschap Production.'

He snatched up the phone, about to dial the number Al had given him as his office, when he hesitated. His heart pounded with excitement. It was perfect. But perhaps he ought to wait. Wait until the script came in. But wouldn't this help them with the script? If they had an opening like that? A sock opening? He decided to wait and write it down, get the music written as well. Present Al with the whole package. That would prove to them that he had something more than integrity to contribute to the series.

He scrabbled about in his desk drawer for music paper. He thought he had some but wasn't quite sure.

'If you're looking for your aspirin bottle, I have it,' Evelyn said.

'No,' Julius said. 'I was looking for some music paper I thought I put away.'

'Oh, my God,' Evelyn said wearily. 'What happened at lunch?'

'Oh, we have a deal,' Julius said. 'Al and I shook hands on it.'

'That's nice,' Evelyn said. 'And did he slip you any money?'

'Well, no, not yet.'

'Did he give you a contract to sign?'

'We shook hands,' Julius said sturdily.

'So what? I shake hands with lots of people. So far I haven't gotten anything from it but a skin rash.'

'There are certain kinds of people you can shake hands with and that's agreement enough,' Julius explained.

'Oh, my God,' Evelyn said. 'Well, there's one consolation. There's nothing he can take from you. If he has a money machine that makes ten-dollar bills out of singles, don't go to the bank with him before you let me in on it.'

'He's a legitimate producer,' Julius said stubbornly. 'And what's more, an honest man.'

'If I ever saw a thief, he's a thief. The little one is too nervous to be a thief. But that big one can steal the bowels out of your rear end if you bend over to pick up a nickel.'

'Al Douglas is an honest man, Evelyn!'

'Ha, ha,' Evelyn said flatly.

Seymour Waxler entered the office. Evelyn turned back to her typewriter. Waxler's yellow-brown eyes darted about. He cleared his throat. 'Is Mr Pollack in?'

'No, he's out,' Evelyn said, typing busily.

Waxler looked about. 'Do you expect him back soon?'

'Gone for the day,' Evelyn said laconically.

'I'd like to make an appointment,' Waxler finally said.

'Sorry. Mr Pollack makes his own appointments,' Evelyn went on, not looking up from her typewriter.

Julius looked up from his search, his heart touched by the sound of Seymour Waxler's voice. 'Hello, Seymour,' Julius said.

'Hello,' Waxler said stuffily. 'He never seems to be in when I call.'

'Tough,' Evelyn said.

'I've been thinking that perhaps we ought to have a written contract on this matter. I've written to the Dramatists Guild.'

'Good idea,' Evelyn replied.

'I mean, if Mr Pollack wants to option the play –' Waxler said, and cleared his throat again.

'If you have any other offers,' Evelyn said calmly as she looked up, 'take my advice, take them.'

'Did Mr Pollack say that?' Waxler asked, the note of dismay in his voice hurting Julius.

'No, Mr Pollack did not say that. I say that,' Evelyn replied.

'Well, you'll forgive me, miss,' Waxler said, clearing his throat furiously, 'but I don't think you know what you're talking about.'

'I don't forgive you,' Evelyn said, picking up the phone. 'Because I know what I'm talking about.'

Waxler's eyes shifted unhappily. 'Do you think so, Julius?' Waxler asked.

'Don't ask him,' Evelyn said crisply. 'He's a bigger sleep-walker than you.'

'Have faith in your talent,' Julius said fervently, intensely. 'It's a wonderful play, Seymour. It nearly made me cry.'

'Does Mr Pollack think so, too?' Waxler asked.

'Oh, yes, he does, he does, Seymour,' Julius cried out.

'He hasn't read it,' Evelyn said coldly.

'I don't believe that,' Waxler replied. He looked to Julius.

'Mr Pollack doesn't like to read plays before they're finished,' Julius explained. 'He feels that that way he doesn't let the imperfections get in the way of what he knows the playwright will ultimately produce.'

'He hasn't read my rewrites?' Waxler asked, and this time the throat clearing sounded suspiciously like tears being choked back.

'Oh, yes, yes, he does read them!' Julius said, feeling his own tears about to fall.

'Mr Pollack reads nothing but the dinner menu,' Evelyn said, dialling the phone.

'Tell him I came to see him,' Waxler said in an oddly

muffled and strangled voice as he turned and left quickly.

Evelyn looked up from the phone and saw Julius. Her lips pursed. 'Don't you dare cry,' she said bitterly. But it was too late.

Hanrahan observed Daphne carefully. 'If your father won't be back, perhaps you can help me.'

'Perhaps I can,' she said with a smooth smile.

'Are you a member of the Truth Seekers?'

'Yes,' she replied.

Hanrahan nodded. It ran to a pattern in these crank organizations. 'Could you give me a list of your members?'

'We don't have any list,' Daphne said.

'You could give me, instead, the names and addresses of the principal officers?'

'I could. But I won't,' Daphne replied with a smile.

Hanrahan nodded wearily. That, too, ran to a pattern. 'I can apply for a court order,' Hanrahan said with a profound sense that what he was saying was so much of a formula that the words had no meaning for him. They meant nothing to him because they were too familiar. Obviously they fell on the ears of others as fresh words, fresh combinations, provocative, stimulating, exciting, even frightening.

'And if the court orders, then what?' Daphne asked.

'If you still refuse, you will be in contempt of court and can be sentenced to imprisonment.'

Again, Hanrahan thought. Again the formulas. Again the words that really meant nothing.

'I have been in prison before. It doesn't interest me,' Daphne said.

Hanrahan looked at her. That's hard to believe, kid.

Have you? Well, perhaps you have. Putting you in prison doesn't interest me, either. You and I are doing a sort of dance together, aren't we? You step one way and I step another. A contra-dance. But the dance, for me, is so flat and stale and profitless. Why be stubborn? Stop the dance and behave yourself. The dance has never led anyone anywhere but to prison, and in the end the lists were produced and checked and the results were always stale and academic. He recalled the guardian of a list that contained the names of Loyalist supporters. They had fought for five years to get the lists. And they got them. And it meant nothing. The Spanish Civil War was long gone. Even Franco was bored with the subject. The night of terror the guardian was holding back wasn't really a night of terror at all. It wasn't even an overcast afternoon, except in the minds of those who lived in a dream of terror.

'I'll make a note of that,' Hanrahan said, and made a mysterious note on his paper. And that's nonsense, too, kid. Just a little way of scaring you. Please be scared a little and get this over with. Be reasonable. But then, if you were reasonable you wouldn't belong to a crank organization. That's what makes cranks. They are stubborn dreamers.

The door opened and Julius entered.

Hanrahan looked him over carefully and liked him at once. Julius glanced at Hanrahan and crossed to Daphne. Hanrahan observed the way in which Daphne floated into the young man's arms. He observed, too, the way in which Julius moved slightly away from her. Hanrahan smiled. So that's the way it is.

'Are you a Truth Seeker, too?' Hanrahan asked.

'Well, yes,' Julius said uncertainly.

'Aren't you sure?' Hanrahan asked.

'I want to be truthful about it,' Julius said solemnly.

'The fact of the matter is that I'm not sure whether I'm acceptable to Mr Leydecker or the rest of the group. I'd like to be – for Daphne's sake,' Julius said tenderly. She gave him a melting look.

'And what's your name?' Hanrahan asked.

'Julius Schapiro,' he said.

'Oh, we have you,' Hanrahan said a little wearily.

'He's from the Secret Service,' Daphne said. 'Tell him nothing.'

'Really?!' Julius exclaimed, and the look of delight and surprise and awe in his face amused Hanrahan.

'How many members are there in the Truth Seekers organization?' Hanrahan asked.

'Tell him nothing,' Daphne replied.

'Why not?' Julius asked. 'After all, if we're Truth Seekers we ought to be able to tell the truth about ourselves. Let me see.' Julius thought for a moment. 'About eight of us that I know, and I include myself in that. Although, strictly speaking, I'm not yet a member.'

'Eight?' Hanrahan asked. No, that can't be. It can't be that small. I didn't expect it to be very large. But eight is simple foolishness.

'Ten,' Daphne said, as if sensing what Hanrahan's thoughts were. 'There are two sisters who are too sick to attend meetings. We go to their apartment twice a month.'

'And the reason you wouldn't give me the list of officers was because everyone's an officer?' Hanrahan said with a smile. Daphne rewarded him with a dazzling smile. Hanrahan shook his head pityingly.

'Mr Leydecker says that he never expects the organization to grow very large,' Julius said earnestly. 'He says that we – they are an *élite* group.'

'Most likely you are,' Hanrahan said. 'But the government of the United States isn't interested in *élite* groups.

Only in plebeian groups. Large groups. Are any members of your group employees of the federal government?'

'I'm not,' Julius said, and looked to Daphne.

'I don't think so,' Daphne replied. 'In any case, I won't tell you. Get your court order first. Send us to jail.'

'Do you want to go to jail, Mr Schapiro?' Hanrahan asked.

'Some of the best people in the world's history have been in jail,' Julius replied a bit grandly.

Hanrahan smiled. I'll bet he's read that somewhere. 'I suppose you're right, historically speaking. But that's only historically.'

'I beg your pardon?' Julius asked, puzzled.

'Historically the best people have landed in jails. Not lately. You would be in jail with some fairly common criminals. We haven't put a truly distinguished man or woman behind bars in over fifty years.'

'Then we'll break that tradition for you,' Daphne said sweetly.

Hanrahan looked first at one and then at the other.

'Do either of you really want to go to jail? I mean, speaking quite seriously.'

Julius hesitated, and Hanrahan felt the truth coming from Julius. No, not you, kid. I can feel that. And how about you, blondie? You really don't care, do you? You might even enjoy it. 'Well,' Hanrahan said, rising, 'I'll come back when Mr Leydecker is here. Meanwhile, I'll get the court order.' He put on his hat, looked at the two young people, and went out.

Daphne was in his arms the moment the door clicked shut.

'He means it,' Julius said soberly. 'I don't particularly want to go to jail.'

'Oh, it can be fun,' Daphne said intimately, and nuzzled his ear.

'I couldn't bear the idea of your being in jail,' Julius said, kissing her eyelid.

'Perhaps they'll put us together,' she said softly, wickedly.

'They won't,' Julius said morosely, and wondered what his mother would think if he went to prison. Prison seemed such a dreary, cold and cheerless place. The food would be bad and the toilet facilities primitive. And what would happen to his association with Mr Douglas and Mr Cohen? Wouldn't that, of necessity, have to be abandoned? And his job with Mr Pollack? Mr Pollack would understand, but Evelyn would think him a fool. And did he want to go to jail for being a Truth Seeker? Was he a Truth Seeker? If he refused, what would Daphne think of him? Would she regard him a coward? A deserter? 'I have something to ask you,' Julius said, looking at her.

'Yes,' she replied dreamily. 'Yes, yes, yes.'

'I'm not speaking of that!' Julius cried out a little peevishly. My God, what's wrong with her? Is she in love with me or is she just uncontrollable?

'I don't care what you want,' Daphne replied. 'The answer is yes.' Her tongue touched the inside of his ear.

A swift thrill of excited embarrassment ran through him. 'Daphne, please be serious.'

'Oh, you monk!' she cried out, and pulled him down on the couch.

He sat beside her, trying to avoid her gliding hands.

'If I am a Truth Seeker –'

'Yes,' she said irrelevantly, opening the buttons of his shirt.

'I ought to stick by the organization, shouldn't I?' he said, trying to button up the buttons she had opened. He started slightly as he felt her hand under his undershirt.

'Of course,' she murmured, opening his belt.

'But am I a Truth Seeker?' he asked, closing his belt at the same time he fought her hand over his zipper.

'Welcome to the membership,' she said, and lunged on him, tearing open his zipper.

'You're hopeless!' he cried in excited horror at the swift and sure way she had found him.

'Helpless,' she corrected, her lips on his.

'Let me help you,' he said, helplessly, as he fumbled with her dress. She waited and when she was sure she smiled and let him help her.

It was wrong, Julius thought helplessly. Wrong. Wrong.

He left in the early darkest hours of the morning. He had never stayed so late and he wondered what his mother would think. He gasped with surprise when a man fell in step beside him. His muscles froze as he considered whether to fight or run.

'Evening, Mr Schapiro,' the man said, and Julius realized with a greater shock that it was the Secret Service man.

'Have – have you been waiting all this time?' Julius asked shakily.

'Don't apologize,' Hanrahan said with a smile. 'She's a lovely girl.'

'We – we talked.'

'Of course,' Hanrahan said politely.

'Miss Leydecker and I are going to be married,' Julius said, realizing now that the lights had been out in the apartment most of the night. A fact the Secret Service man could have easily checked.

'Congratulations,' Hanrahan said, and meant it. If she was a crank, she was a lovely crank, and marriage settled women down. 'All the more reason I'm glad I waited to talk to you privately.'

'What about?' Julius asked and realized instantly he knew. He was going to be asked to be an informer.

'What sort of a man is her father, Mr Leydecker?'

'He's a man of great integrity,' Julius said, determined not to give this minion of the government the slightest scrap of information that would be useful to him.

They stopped. 'This is my car,' Hanrahan explained. 'Can I take you home?'

Julius hesitated. Would the favour compromise him? He decided not, and they got in.

Hanrahan said little as they drove through the darkened streets. 'You know, Mr. Schapiro,' Hanrahan said casually, 'we meet up with lots of odd people in our business,'

'I'm sure you do,' Julius said primly.

'Take these crank organizations, for instance. I'll be frank with you and take the chance of offending you – but this group, the Truth Seekers, they're a bunch of cranks.'

'If you think so,' Julius agreed.

'Harmless, for the most part. Now and then we run into an action group and they can be dangerous. That's why we check them all out.'

'I presume the truth can be dangerous,' Julius said. Let him have it. Show him that you're no one's fool. Sooner or later he's going to tip his hand. If he could only time it so that he could whip out the refusal gracefully, for instance, as he slammed the door shut in his face.

'Oh, hell, we don't worry about the truth,' Hanrahan said. 'That's all relative. No, I mean, these organizations with generalized grievances. They're okay so long as they belly-ache about everything. But somewhere along the line they go sour. They get specific. And when they get specific they sometimes try specific methods.'

'Such as?'

'Violence. Gathering petitions is one thing. Nothing to worry us about that. But one day gathering petitions doesn't seem active enough and someone proposes the making of a bomb.'

'Oh, so now I'm a bomb thrower, eh?' Julius asked with a superior smile. Why were these government men so predictable?

'No, I don't think you are. Making a bomb takes fairly complex technical skill. It's not something you can buy. And if it's not done properly, there's more danger to the maker than there is to the intended victim.'

'We're not making bombs,' Julius said.

'No. Not now. But the time may come when you will. It would be helpful if I knew whether anyone in the group has the skill to make one. For instance, is there anyone in the group who is a machinist?'

'I'm sure I don't know.'

'But you could find out,' Hanrahan said with a smile.

There it was, Julius thought. Naked. Out in the open. And they were nowhere near his home. 'I suppose I could. But I wonder if I should.' Julius said, tantalizingly.

'Oh, hell, I could find out fast enough if I wanted to,' Hanrahan said genially.

'I see. But you don't want to,' Julius replied with an air of superiority. This fellow was truly crude.

'I'd have to get a court order and your fiancée looks crank enough to refuse, and I'd have to put her in jail. I don't want to.'

Julius's brows knit. He had not thought of that. 'Why would you have to pick on her? Why not her father? He got her into it.'

'Sure. But if I know her father, he won't be home again. He'll hide out and leave her behind.'

'He wouldn't do that,' Julius said, uncertainly. The

man who let her be sold into slavery? Come on now, Julius. Don't be a fool. Leydecker certainly would.

'Oh, he'll probably feel that we'd hesitate to act against a girl as young and sweet as that. But the government isn't much for youth or sweetness, Mr Schapiro.' Hanrahan fixed his eyes on Julius when they stopped at a light. 'We're all human in the department. There's not a man I know who wouldn't help her as much as he could. But we can't act as individuals. We have to act as arms of the federal government. Once they refuse the court's order, it becomes automatic, blind. I'd like to see your girl saved from the automatic machinery of the department. It's brutal.'

Julius looked at Hanrahan. There was something blunt and kindly in his tired face, and his voice gave Julius the feeling that he was genuine, honest. 'Do you mean that?' Julius asked cautiously.

'About wanting to help her? Sure,' Hanrahan said. 'Hell, why cause more suffering than you have to. Look, Mr Schapiro, you don't think I want to do my job the hard way, do you? I don't mean the hard way for me. It would be the easy way for me to do it – court order, hearing, sentencing, let them stew in jail a while and then get the membership list. We'll get it, you know. Nothing's ever stopped us before. It won't stop us now.'

'She's innocent, you know,' Julius said. 'I mean, if you knew the way her father's raised her –'

'I can guess. I know these cranks. They ruin their own families first. I've seen it a dozen times. Sweet girls turned into sour embittered old maids because their fathers wouldn't let go of them.'

No, but her trouble has been that her father has never trained her, instilled in her the respect for morals. But wasn't it the same thing? Merely the other side of the coin? 'What do you want to know?' Julius said a little breathily. He had agreed to come in. In a darkened car speeding through the deserted streets of the lower Bronx he had sold out. The Judas with his thirty pieces of silver. Only he wasn't doing it for money. He was doing it for Daphne's sake. So this is how traitors are made? The informer. That's what he was. The informer.

As he snuggled down under his blankets that night, he tried not to think of what he had agreed to do. Mr Hanrahan had made it sound innocent enough, innocuous enough. But wasn't the truth branded on his skin like a livid scar? He was an informer. He shuddered with deep shame. He loved Daphne too much. Honour meant nothing to him. How did it go? I would love thee yet if I did not love honour more. That was poetry. That was about a real hero. But he was not a real hero. Not a real hero at all. Oh, Daphne, see what you've made me do? Oh, my God, Julius Schapiro is a fink. Go to sleep, fink. Go to sleep. And, with a shudder, he did.

Hanrahan, half a city away, sat on the edge of his bed, almost too tired to sleep. The waiting had exhausted him. He was forty-six, too old for this sort of business. Why was he bothering? What would kids like that ever do? They would do what they did while he was standing in a doorway waiting. That's all they would ever do. Lucky bastard, Schapiro. She was a knockout. But young enough to be your daughter. If I had a wife. And if she had had a child. And if that child had been girl. Why not a wife? No. Not the fat, simpering empty-headed colleens he met at the Irish-American dances. And not the thick-ankled ignorant widows his mother archly paraded for him. And how about the honest, hard-working females in the office? God, what monsters! It wasn't that he wanted a pretty woman. Normal looking. He was, himself, no beauty. Merely normal looking. But not a lump of meal. Not a dough-faced biddy filled with the prattle of holiness, the cackle of joy over a nephew who was a priest or about to become one. Not those. He'd go to hell unshriven rather than marry one of those. In confession Hanrahan was truculent — when he went. The priest always sensed it. 'And what of your sin of pride, my son?' Hanrahan's shoulders squared. Hell, yes, pride. He was proud and he was damned if he considered it a sin. Maybe coveting Schapiro's girl was a sin. Maybe. Lying to Schapiro was not a sin. That fell into the category of rendering unto Caesar what was Caesar's. Dispensation granted for the disability of his profession. Professional liar. Professional bully. Professional snooper. Professional voyeur. Only the bricks of the building and the feebleness of his eyes kept him from watching those two kids. Anything to relieve the monotony of standing and waiting. Nauseating specimen, Hanrahan, aren't you? You old bastard. Would you have watched if you had the chance? No, I'm too proud. The hell you are. You're too hungry. Hunger takes away pride. Even yours. Even mine? Then why haven't I chosen the likeliest of the acceptable women and have done with it? Because they sicken you. The only thing that would solve it would be a perpetual erection and a bottomless sack. Which I ain't got, Hanrahan said half aloud with a rueful grin. The only thing I want is an honest woman. Oh, God, for an honest woman. Someone to talk to. Someone just to talk to.

'Out of the ages,' Julius sang as he played the piano. 'Torn from the pages/The mysteries of the sages/The passions and the rages/We are the seekers,' he closed his eyes for the effect and then, too, because people sitting in the lobby of the hotel were watching him. He did not want to see Al's face. Not until he was done with it. 'The word/The word of truth!' Julius concluded with a strong resolving chord, and opened his eyes. He looked anxiously at Al Douglas's face and then at Lou Cohen.

Al Douglas nodded heavily. 'That's it. That's it. You feel it, too, Lou?'

'Beef it up with an orchestration maybe,' Lou Cohen said dubiously.

'No! No!' Al cried. 'Jesus! Don't you see it with a drum and maybe a guitar? Christ! I see it!'

Julius, who was about to agree with Lou Cohen about a full orchestra suddenly found himself in agreement with Al. That was the idea. Stark simplicity. He was grateful he had not spoken too soon.

An officious-looking man with a flower in his buttonhole approached them. 'I'm sorry,' he said with mean firmness, 'but this piano is not for public use.'

'That's all right,' Al said breezily. 'We're done with it.'

'You gentlemen don't happen to be guests of this hotel, do you?' the man with the flower in his buttonhole asked suspiciously.

'I wouldn't stay in this –' Al began, but he was cut

off at once by the man with the flower in his button-hole.

'That will be quite enough. Now' – he lowered his bullet-shaped head slightly to match the faint dropping of his voice – 'you will leave at once or I shall call the police.'

Before Al could reply, Lou Cohen slipped in, as neatly and deftly as a razor blade. 'Sure, mister. No harm done. Just an expression of art. We're going right now. This minute. No charge for the entertainment either.'

Julius felt his elbow gripped strongly by Lou Cohen's bony fingers and he was propelled out of the lobby onto the street in all of its spring luncheon brightness.

'Why must it always be an argument?' Lou Cohen asked his partner querulously. 'You use the man's piano. Be at least polite.'

'I can't stand those creeps with funeral flowers in their coats,' Al Douglas said, biting into the end of a fresh cigar. 'Remind me the next time we need a suite. I don't want that dump.'

'I'll remind you,' Lou Cohen said with a faint sigh.

'You really like it, Al?' Julius asked as he dodged the oncoming crowd to fall in beside Douglas.

'Baby, it was just right. It was an inspiration. I didn't know you wrote music, too.'

Julius was about to confess but shame overcame him. 'I write a lot of music.'

'That's where the real money is,' Lou Cohen said with a sigh.

'No reason why we couldn't cut a record of the theme,' Al said, pausing to light his cigar while they waited for a traffic light.

'After we get the pilot in the can,' Lou Cohen said.

'Why wait until then? We're still three months away from production.'

'Is it that close?' Julius asked, surprised, accustomed to the long production dates of plays.

'Baby,' Al Douglas said, 'I told you I was hot for this one, didn't I? As soon as we have the script, we go. I've got the studio space right now. You put down a hold on it, Lou, didn't you?'

'I have a definite hold,' Lou said.

'Once we have the script in our hands, we start casting. Joe is standing by.'

'Joe?' Julius asked.

'You don't know Joe?' Al asked, astonished.

'One of the best directors in the business,' Lou Cohen said. 'Used to work for deMille.'

'*Work* for deMille?' Al said, eyeing a girl walking towards them. 'He *did* deMille's pictures. You don't believe all that hooey about deMille with the megaphone and the riding boots, do you? Joe did it all. Don't let anyone kid you. Okay, baby,' Al said as he stopped. 'We got to leave you here. Unless you want to have a drink with us before lunch?'

'We won't have time, Al,' Lou Cohen said fussily, checking his watch.

'Listen, we have time, Lou. We have time. What are they? CBS network brass? Crap on them. Julie's a partner.'

'I wouldn't want to hold you up, Al,' Julius said gratefully. 'After all,' he said perkily, 'they might buy our show.'

Al Douglas laughed richly. 'You hear that, Lou? Takes to the business like a fish to water. Slides right in there, doesn't he? Maybe we ought to take him along?'

Lou Cohen's eyes slid helplessly from side to side.

'No, I better get back to the office. Mr Pollack will be looking for me when he comes in.'

'A nice Jewish kid,' Al Douglas said warmly, and put

his bearlike arm around Julius's shoulders and squeezed him affectionately. 'If Estelle had only had a kid. He would have been like you.'

'Estelle?' Julius asked politely.

'My goddamned ex-wife,' Al Douglas said cheerfully.

'Now, let's not start on Estelle,' Lou Cohen said nervously, and held out his wrist watch for Al's attention.

'Give me that song again, kid,' Al said.

Julius began to hum it.

'With the words, baby,' Al said.

'Out of the ages,' Julius sang, waving his hand in the air to keep the tempo. 'Torn from the pages/The mysteries of the sages/The passions and the rages/We are the seekers –'

Al had picked it up now and was repeating it, his huge, meaty fist dangerously punching the air for tempo and emphasis.

'The word, the word, the word of truth!' Julius finished.

'The word, the word, the word of truth!' Al bellowed, startling passers-by even in that noisy throng. Although none of the startled ones hesitated when they saw Al's size and the size of the fist he brandished. They swallowed their curiosity and hurried on.

Lou Cohen took the opportunity of a traffic light to push his partner. Julius watched them cross Sixth Avenue. Al Douglas's huge figure weaving in time to the music, his enormous clenched paw chopping and hooking in the air as he sang and kept time. Lou Cohen followed, dogging him, a sallow shadow, nervous, thin, and hurried. Julius watched them until the flow of traffic obliterated them from sight. He hurried back to the office, humming to himself.

Julius's buoyancy disappeared when he saw Hanrahan in the office. What was he to do? What protocol could he follow? Should he ignore Hanrahan? Pretend he didn't know him? Why hadn't they discussed that vital matter when they had met a week before? Hanrahan took the problem out of his hands.

'Hello, Julius,' Hanrahan said in a friendly fashion.

'Oh, hello, Mr. Hanrahan,' Julius said, flustered, wondering what Evelyn knew.

'I haven't heard from you in a week so I thought I'd drop by,' Hanrahan said. *In case you had some information for me.*

Julius panicked. Did he say that? No, of course not. He had merely finished the sentence for him. Not in front of Evelyn. She was a witch. She could read minds.

'I'd like to –' Julius stopped, considering how best to speak to Hanrahan privately. Hanrahan waited, smiling slightly. Why, in God's name, was he so stupid? Why wasn't he helping. Didn't he know the elementals of undercover work? What ruse could he devise to get Hanrahan out of the office so that they might speak without being overheard? Especially by Evelyn. 'I have a luncheon appointment. I'm sorry. Perhaps if you could come back after lunch,' Julius muttered vaguely, and hurried out of the office. His best bet was to wait for Hanrahan outside of the building and discreetly follow him until, unobserved, he could fall in behind him and whisper a quick word to him. Obviously if Hanrahan didn't know his job, it had to be done for him. He could see the bewildered Hanrahan. 'Very neat, kid,' Hanrahan would say. 'You've got a real instinct for this kind of work. Maybe I'd better talk to the chief about you. Would our kind of work interest you?' Julius considered it for a moment. Would it? Flying back and forth between two continents, code words, countersigns, disguises, poisoned capsules hidden inside the cheek in case of a dangerous interception. There would be women, of course. There always were. Parisian gamins with apartments of their own. Cool English ladies with their tweeds and candid hazel eyes. Not so cool without their tweeds and with their frank hazel eyes. Brazen hazel eyes. Hazel eyes. It had a cool sound. You bewitched me with your hazel eyessss ... yes, you did, you did. Enchanted me with hazel eyessss ... those eyes, those eyes ... In the cool English rain ... that floated from Spain ... I felt the sweet pain ... of those eyes, hazel eyes! Hazel eyessss!

'Funny kid,' Hanrahan said to Evelyn.

'A sleep-walker,' Evelyn said. 'He's been in and out of here twice this morning. I admit we don't do a lot of work around here. But we do keep up appearances. He's fallen to pieces.'

'How so?' Hanrahan asked, crossing his legs and taking out his cigarettes.

'Ever since his name appeared nationally. Julius has always been a dreamer of one kind or another. Now the Jewish Mau Maus are after him.' Evelyn took one of Hanrahan's cigarettes and accepted a light.

'The Jewish Mau Maus,' Hanrahan said with a smile, liking Evelyn even more than he had after they had spent twenty minutes together before Julius's arrival.

'Oh, the head-hunters who run through these jungles trying to make a buck. Either with your skin or mine. But never theirs. He's got two pests named Douglas and Cohen working up a TV-film series about the Truth Seekers. Nothing will come of it. I've seen it happen before. Christ, it happens right here, all the time. Pollack has done it a hundred times, and Julius has watched it happen and he hasn't learned.' She shook her head sadly as she exhaled and scraped the ash from her cigarette.

'It hurts when people don't learn, doesn't it?' Hanrahan asked, fully understanding.

'I don't expect people to learn a goddamn thing,'

Evelyn said crisply. 'They never disappoint me. But once in a while, you get a feeling for one of the sleep-walkers and you wish, somehow, you could awaken them.'

'Like Julius?

'He's a decent kid,' Evelyn said with a soft smile. Hanrahan noted the smile and liked that, too. 'Maybe they're all decent. I don't know. I make it my business not to find out. I've got enough heartaches dealing with the sleep-walkers God dealt me as relatives. Why strain yourself picking up strangers?'

'Yes, of course,' Hanrahan said, smoking and watching and liking.

'You're a cute one,' Evelyn observed flatly.

'How so?'

'You're working so goddamned hard at being a Secret Service man. You say four words and I say fifty.'

Hanrahan smiled. 'I don't mean it that way. I find your views refreshing.'

'In a pig's eye you do,' Evelyn said with a smile. 'You hope I'll spill my guts about Julius. All right, I will. Take out your notebook and write it down. He's a kid. A sweet, dumb, innocent kid. He lives with his mouth open. It's just one great big beautiful world to him. He's a sleep-walker and a mouth breather. So write that down in your book for the other clucks in the Secret Service to figure out.'

'I knew that the minute I met him,' Hanrahan said. 'And not all of us are clucks.'

'I don't know,' Evelyn said, watching Hanrahan through her harlequin glasses. 'Talk to me a little.'

'I'd rather listen,' Hanrahan said.

'Some people have a gift for listening. They can listen with such intelligence that it fools you. The minute they stop listening and start talking I begin to hear it: Cluck . . . cluck . . . cluck.'

'Yes,' Hanrahan chuckled. 'I know exactly what you mean. I've seen it happen – lots of times. But what can you do about it?'

'Note for future reference,' Evelyn said, snuffing out the cigarette firmly.

'What if all your life you had to deal with such people,' Hanrahan said speculatively.

'I've had to. I get along.'

'Not by puncturing them all the time.'

'All the time. Everytime,' Evelyn said sharply.

Hanrahan looked at her with increased respect. 'Are you married?'

'No. Nor ever have.'

'Nor will be?' Hanrahan suggested mildly.

'Nor will be,' Evelyn said, and the note of unhappiness was in her voice. 'But hope to be,' Evelyn went on. 'You see, I'm a little of a sleep-walker myself. You have to be. Or you become a crank. Like the Truth Seekers and they turn out to be the biggest sleep-walkers of all.'

'But surely there are men in the world who would appreciate a woman like you.' Hanrahan said with surprise.

'Mr Hanrahan, people smell roses. They don't wrap their arms around rose bushes.'

'But the thorns are merely to protect the sweetness,' Hanrahan said.

'I've got too many thorns and I smell only up close. Very close,' Evelyn said dryly.

'How close?'

'To my husband I'll smell sweet,' Evelyn said.

'But you should smell sweet to a lover before he becomes a husband,' Hanrahan observed.

Evelyn looked at him sharply. 'Mr Hanrahan, my first job came when I was nineteen. I had a little fanny and two sweet little boobies and I was too vain to wear glasses for my astigmatism. As a result my eyes had that liquid, melting look all nearsighted people have. And all sorts of candidates were touching my fanny and bumping my boobies and smelling me very thoroughly. But with my nearsighted eyes I couldn't tell much. So I fought back and the closer they came the harder I fought and finally scared off most of them to the point where they were oblong blurs in sharkskin, mohair, and English wool. By the time I was twenty-eight I decided it was time to see just who was doing the pinching and bumping and the smelling. And when I could see them I didn't like them any better. My tongue got sharper and my fanny got bigger and my boobies got heavier. Today I wear wonderful glasses, an expensive full corset, and I know what the hell I want. The hell of it is – I can't see it. And if I did – it wouldn't see me.'

'I feel very lucky,' Hanrahan said with a smile.

'I see you very clearly, Hanrahan,' Evelyn said. 'To me so far you look like no lover and no potential husband.'

'Then get your glasses changed. To me you look like the reason I'm a forty-six-year-old bachelor who's giving up.'

'Giving up what?'

'Being a bachelor.' Hanrahan rose. 'Are you free for lunch, may I ask?'

'Are you inviting me to lunch?'

'Yes,' Hanrahan said.

Evelyn rose and stood straight, looking at Hanrahan. 'Take a good look, Hanrahan. I'm fat, in my forties, and independent.'

'Yes, so I see,' Hanrahan said tenderly. 'May I have the honour of taking you to lunch?'

'I'll get my hat.'

Julius's heart leaped when he saw Hanrahan and then stopped short, frozen when he saw that Evelyn's hand was tucked cosily under his arm. They were talking and smiling at one another and were oblivious of him although they could have seen him by the slightest movement of their eyes. They walked out into the spring sunshine.

Julius hurried to the apartment for the meeting of the Truth Seekers. Perhaps the last meeting, if he understood Daphne's call. His mother had answered the phone and had started probing with her. 'And whom is speaking, please? Miss Leydecker? Oh, I see. Yes, indeed. And you wish to speak to my son – Julius? Is this in reference to his availability this evening? Oh, yes, I see. Indeed I see.' It could have gone on remorselessly for another twenty minutes if Julius had not taken the phone from his mother's hand. Mrs Schapiro had favoured her son with a I'll-talk-to-you-later look. But Daphne's remarks had so rattled him that he hurried out of his apartment without giving his mother a chance to speak to him. He knew that it meant that she would nag him for a week but he had to take that risk. Mr Hanrahan ought to have been notified but he was beginning to feel annoyed with the Secret Service man. He had taken Evelyn to lunch and to dinner as well. He had, in fact, seen more of Evelyn than he had of Julius. What was the matter with the guy? Didn't he want the information? What a hell of a way to run a secret service! No wonder the Russians had that terrible lead over the U.S. Depend on Hanrahan and see how far back it pushes you.

When Julius arrived, most of the Truth Seekers were already there, including the two elderly sisters Julius had heard about but whom he had never met. Daphne winked at him. It was a promise about later. Julius swallowed hard. He would never really understand her.

The man with the spiky hair and loud shoes was not wearing his usual work clothes. Instead, he was dressed neatly in a clean suit, his spiky hair unsuccessfully combed down with hair tonic. He needed a shave but not badly. He smoked a cheap cigar. The fat man with sighs draped his arm over the couch where he sat and surveyed the company benignly. The young man with the beard was there alone. His woman was elsewhere. Perhaps still escaping from him. The lady thin as a slat still was thin and she had now taken up knitting and had given up writing in a child's copybook. The huge granitic secretary was still huge, still granitic. The elderly sisters, looking like dusty English sparrows, sat together, looking about with wet, uncertain old women's eyes. Leydecker, firm, well-fleshed, clean, and square, occupied the chair at the dining-room table, which had been brought into the living-room. When Julius came into the room and slipped into his chair, Leydecker rapped the table.

'We will dispense with the reading of the minutes,' Leydecker said.

The man with the spiky hair nodded his head agreeably and blew a smoke ring.

'Since our last meeting, a number of things have happened. Some of you know of our arrest by the police because you were, yourselves, arrested. Some of you were fortunate enough to have escaped arrest, and some of you' – here he inclined his head towards the two dusty sisters – 'could not join us for reasons of health. While our demonstration in mid-town Manhattan two months ago was not successful in raising the required number of signatures for our petitions, it did succeed in giving our organization national prominence. And, of course, as you all know, whenever an organization receives public attention it comes under investigation. We have come under investigation.'

There was a definite stir of interest. The man with the spiky hair took his cigar out of his mouth and leaned forward. The fat sighing man stopped sighing and stared at Leydecker. The young man with a beard made a fuss about lighting a cigarette, and it was clear to Julius that the fuss was made to cover his alarm.

'Investigation by whom?' the thin slat of a woman said, her knitting halted, the needles poised towards one another.

'By the Secret Service.'

The stir was stronger now. The man with the noisy shoes rose from his chair, his mouth half opened to speak.

'Now, please,' Leydecker said, holding up a square hand. 'Allow me to finish what I have to say on the matter and then I shall be pleased to throw the floor open to any questions or comments you care to make.' When he was sure he had their attention, he continued. 'Evidently the Secret Service began its real investigation when it received an anonymous letter denouncing the group as communistic, radical, subversive, and of great danger to the republic.'

Now they began to mutter to themselves and to one another. Julius was puzzled. He had assumed that the item in the national magazine had brought Hanrahan into the case. What letter was this?

'Anonymous, hunh?' the man with the spiky hair said harshly. Then he turned and looked at Julius. Julius felt himself stiffen.

'The Secret Service,' Leydecker went on, 'has demanded the membership list. That demand was put to my daughter. She, quite naturally, refused. She was told that a court order would be obtained and that if we still failed to produce the membership list, we would be found in contempt of court and sent to jail.'

'Fascists!' the man with the beard said and rose. 'I have something to say –'

'Please,' Leydecker said, 'when I am through.' The young man with the beard did not sit down. He walked to the window, smoking furiously. 'Now, the Secret Service already knows the names of everyone here.'

Now there were gasps, and the dusty sisters looked as though they were going to rise but their wings appeared too short and feeble to make the flight. As a result, they seemed to be making brief, ineffectual hops from their chairs and falling back in frustration.

'What fink gave it to them?' the man with the spiky hair said, rising menacingly, turning towards Julius. Julius put his hand to his necktie. He hadn't had a chance to tell Hanrahan all of the names since he still did not know all of them. Now some of the others began turning their eyes towards him, and Julius felt trapped. No poison pill in his cheek, no gun in his pocket, he didn't have a chance. While he had no fear of the dusty sisters, Leydecker had always frightened him, the spiky-haired man looked brutal and vicious, and who knew what cruelty the fat sighing man hid behind his innocent flabbiness. Even the sinister needles of the thin slat of a woman would be useful. He winced as he imagined how. Would Daphne raise a finger to save him? Probably not. His body, bruised, broken, punctured by many needle holes would be found in the litter of a partly demolished apartment house. He could see the front-page pictures in the *Daily News*. Police standing about in the amber flicker of emergency lamps, the flash of the police photographer's camera shedding cold light on his broken, crumpled, dusty body. The funeral would be simple, austere.

Pollack in attendance, of course, with Evelyn and his mother, the rabbi, the grave-diggers, Al Douglas and Lou Cohen, perhaps Seymour Waxler ('he was my friend') and – Daphne? Lurking somewhere out of sight would be Hanrahan and his grim-visaged chief. 'I let that kid die,' Hanrahan would say, 'I let him die. Christ, what guts!' Hanrahan would say, and tears would come into his eyes. 'I'll get them,' Hanrahan's words, hard, sharp, bitter, terrible. 'If it's the last thing I ever do, I'll track them down. I'll get every last one of them.' His chief, nodding, would put a commiserative hand on Hanrahan's shoulder. 'We'll all be behind you, fellow. That kid – God, he makes me proud of being an American.' A few months later, in a secret private ceremony in the President's office in the White House, Eisenhower would present his mother with the Congressional Medal of Honour. Mrs. Schapiro, the tears in her eyes, would accept it, and Ike would say: 'We honour your son as an American hero. He fell in the battle that has no banners, no parades, no armies. No fixed battle lines. In that underground war he was one of our great fighters, one of our honoured dead.' In the ante-room of the President's chambers the members of the Washington press would be frustrated, excitedly questioning press secretary Jim Hagerty. But Hagerty could say nothing more than 'It's a private ceremony, boys. I can't tell you more than that. National defence.' 'Give us a break, Jim,' they would cry. 'Why would he get the Congressional Medal of Honour? What did he do? Who was he?' But Hagerty would smile his grim smile and shake his head. 'Sorry, boys. It's a secret. National-defence secret. Top classified matter. I can't tell you more except to say that he earned it. Some day you'll know the truth.' And so the mystery of Julius Schapiro, fallen hero, would rest in history, tantalizing historians, journalists, novelists. Book after book would appear –

The Schapiro Case, *The Unknown Medal of Honour Winner* – and from them would flow plays and movies – *The Man Who Died Alone* – and Douglas and Cohen would prepare a special ninety-minute spectacular on the mysterious case of their hero-partner. Al Douglas, in a severe blue suit, white shirt, would appear before the cameras as the music, in the background, would play his song, 'The Truth Seeker', and would say, 'This is a story of an American hero. He died so that others might live. He gave up no secrets to the enemy. He lived a fantastic adventure. A brief life, to be sure. But a glorious one. I was honoured to know him. His song, "The Truth Seeker", will always be part of the American treasury of songs. But he is not honoured for that. He is being honoured because he did not yield, because he did not give in. His name is Julius Schapiro and this is his story.' Julius leaned back, his eyes half closed, steeling himself for the first levelled charge. He was preparing his answer.

'It does not matter,' Leydecker said, 'just how these names were obtained. We have done nothing contrary to the law and so there is no charge which can be brought against any of us.'

'Charge!' the young man with a beard said disgustedly. 'You don't think they will dare to bring charges against us, do you? No, they'll hound us. They'll get us blacklisted; they'll persecute us over our taxes. They won't come out in the open and accuse us of anything! I say we ought to fight back!'

'That's it!' the man with the spiky hair said. 'Let's fight them!'

'Well, I wonder if that is wise,' Leydecker said, holding up a calming hand. 'After all, we are truth seekers. We want to find the truth for ourselves and so pass on that truth to others.'

'Well, what's the truth about the government case?' the young man with a beard asked.

'The truth is that they have no case,' Leydecker said. 'Now that they have the membership list, they have what they want. My proposal is that we disband the present organization and that each of us goes to different parts of the country as seeds for new chapters. For my daughter and myself, I propose to go to Southern California.'

'What kind of an idea is that?' the man with the spiky hair asked truculently.

'Our founder, Otto Yudiel, wrote in his "Precepts for Truth Seekers" that when the hammer of governmental persecution comes down upon Truth Seekers it should find that Truth Seekers, like mercury, do not crush under the impact, but scatter into bright beads. Each bead to settle elsewhere to grow larger.'

'Yudiel is old-fashioned,' the young man with a beard protested. 'He has no relation with modern times.'

'Sir,' Leydecker said with quiet dignity, 'I shall pretend that I did not hear that slur upon the name of our founder.'

'Bad taste,' the fat sighing man said, shaking his head.

'The slur is doubly reprehensible because we have with us tonight Otto Yudiel's great associate, his life-long partner and friend, the co-founder of our organization, X. F. H.'

There was a gasp of surprise as they looked at one another.

'You mean,' the young man with the beard asked, 'he's here now, among us?'

'He is here in this apartment,' Leydecker said. 'Waiting to join us. To speak to us.' All eyes turned towards the door behind Leydecker. It led to the bedroom.

'I thought X. F. H. was dead,' the thin slat of a woman said, her knitting at an end.

'We have lost touch with him for many years. It was only by the merest stroke of good luck that he contacted us,' Leydecker said.

'Are we sure it is X. F. H.?' the spiky-haired man asked suspiciously.

Leydecker smiled. 'I have spent nearly the whole day with him. He is X. F. H. If he did not look like the many photographs I have seen of him, I would know him. If he did not know ten thousand intimate details of Otto Yudiel's life, I would still know him. He brought me Otto Yudiel's last letters. The handwriting is unmistakable. The contents unmistakable. I also opened the letter which Otto Yudiel gave me on his deathbed. It contained the true identity of X. F. H. There is no mistake. He is X. F. H.'

'A clever disguise could –' the young man with a beard began, but the look on Leydecker's face stopped him.

'Sir, I will not hear any more from you,' Leydecker said severely. He rose. 'I ask you, as homage to this great man, that you all rise.'

They all got to their feet, peering anxiously as Leydecker walked to the bedroom door. Julius, along with the others, craned his neck and waited, his breath in his mouth. He had never heard of X. F. H. except in references during talks. It had never occurred to him that X. F. H. would be a man.

Leydecker opened the door to the bedroom. 'Will you do us the honour of joining us, sir?' Leydecker spoke to the mysterious figure within the next room.

X. F. H. came into the room, following Leydecker, and Julius felt his throat contract with horror. 'I have the

honour,' Leydecker said solemnly, 'to present X. F. H. –
Mr Francis Xavier Hanrahan.'

Hanrahan smiled at them benignly, his eyes twinkling.

Julius looked at Hanrahan with horror and shock and disbelief in his face. He suddenly looked at Daphne, who returned a look of utter smiling blandness.

'It is a pleasure to be with you,' Hanrahan said. 'And I thank Mr Leydecker for extending me the courtesy of attending this meeting. As you know, Otto Yudiel and I were friends for many years. He was a prophet without honour in his own country, and when he came to the United States he lived a life in obscurity. When I first met Otto Yudiel, I was a young police officer. I was, in fact, instrumental in his arrest. I began as Otto Yudiel's arrester and persecutor and I went on to become his friend and his disciple. To some of you it may appear odd or anomalous that a policeman should be a Truth Seeker. But he can be. I was one. Otto Yudiel and I had a difference of opinion in 1930. I believe you now refer to it as the Grand Schism. Otto felt that truth seeking was not an individual matter but a group matter. I felt that each man ought to seek the truth by himself without recourse to groups or organizations. I hold to that belief to this day. I lost touch with Otto as the years went on. I knew that he had gone ahead with groups. I went ahead as an individual. I had hoped that Otto would succeed. Believe me.' Hanrahan put his hand to his breast. 'It was never my mean hope that he would fail. I moved into federal employment and became a member of the United States Secret Service. Across my desk, for many years, flowed the reports on secret organizations within the United States. None of them seemed to have anything to do with Otto Yudiel. I began to feel that he had failed. You can imagine my surprise and delight when I first learned of the Truth Seekers some two months ago. Otto had, after all, not failed. My greatest curiosity lay in finding out how large the group was. I will tell you, frankly, I was disappointed to discover that you numbered merely ten. But ten members can be powerful. I endeavoured to discover the nature of the membership, and today Mr Leydecker spent much of the day discussing the membership with me.'

Julius shook his head in disbelief, his eyes seeking, for his sanity's sake, Daphne's eyes. But she smiled and smiled and offered him no comfort, no anchorage, no reality. How long had she known about it?

'You are the seedbed of Otto Yudiel's dream,' Hanrahan went on calmly. 'As such you owe Otto Yudiel the opportunity of proving that he was right. It was I who suggested to Mr Leydecker that you disperse and each form the nucleus of a new group. Only in that way can you prove that Otto Yudiel was right. Mr Leydecker will discuss with each of you the place where he and I feel you would best do your work. I, of course, hold fast to my own belief. I shall return to my position in the Secret Service and will watch, with interest, your progress. For your sake and for mine, I hope that you do not found any action groups but that you do go ahead in the spirit of the great Otto Yudiel. Thank you.' Hanrahan nodded his head modestly. There was a patter of applause as he sat down and Leydecker took his place.

'I do not propose,' Leydecker said, 'to do more than thank the great teacher, x. f. h., for speaking to us. As Truth Seekers we must find our own way. However, if you feel that Otto Yudiel's vision was a true one, then you must act in accord with the precepts. Those who feel as I do, please raise their hands.'

Almost all of the hands went up except Julius's. He was still too stunned. Hanrahan? A double agent? What was the game here?

'A clear majority,' Leydecker said, satisfied. 'During the course of the week I shall call on each of you for a private discussion concerning your relocation. I know that we shall come to an amicable solution in each case.' He caught the eyes of the fluttering sisters. 'There are those, of course, to whom relocation would be a great hardship – perhaps an insuperable one, and those, of course, are free to remain where they are.' The two sisters subsided and smiled vaguely. 'And that concludes the business of the meeting, unless there are further comments?'

The young man with the beard started to speak but Leydecker firmly brought his hand down on the table. 'Meeting adjourned. There are some refreshments in the kitchen for those who are so inclined.'

Julius at once sought out Daphne and took her aside. 'You knew all the time,' he said, accusingly.

'No, I didn't,' she said with a smile. 'Father told me only this afternoon. I think it's marvellous – don't you?'

'No, I don't,' Julius said, feeling cheated. Hanrahan had made a fool of him. Hadn't he?

'You're coming with us, aren't you?' Daphne said teasingly.

'Where?'

'To Los Angeles. Didn't you hear Father?'

'No, I'm not going to Los Angeles,' Julius said. 'And neither are you.'

'Why, Julius!' Daphne said archly. 'I couldn't stay here alone.'

'You wouldn't be alone,' he said firmly. 'You would have me.'

Leydecker approached him. 'Well,' he said grumpily. 'Get yourself ready, Schapiro.'

'I'm not going, Mr Leydecker,' Julius said.

Leydecker's eyes lit up. 'Well, no need for us to press the matter then. Good luck.'

'Neither is Daphne,' Julius said hurriedly, putting his arm about Daphne. She lounged in the protective circle of his arm and smiled at her father.

'Very well,' Leydecker said after an instant's thought.

'Of course, we'll have the wedding before you leave, Father,' Daphne said.

'Wedding?' Julius echoed, a bit hollowly.

'Wedding?' Leydecker asked curiously. 'Don't tell me you're going to marry him?'

'Yes, of course, Father,' Daphne said soberly.

'Why?' her father asked.

'Because I love him,' Daphne said, tweaking the point of Julius's nose.

'And I thought you had learned something,' Leydecker said disgustedly. 'You're disgustingly bourgeois. Like your mother.'

Julius's eyebrows lifted. Bourgeois? Like her mother?

'You will wear tails, Father, won't you?' Daphne asked coaxingly.

'I will not. The whole bourgeois barbarism of the wedding is too much for my taste. I won't wear the ritual costumes,' Leydecker said.

'If you don't,' she said calmly, 'I won't pay your fare to California.'

'Damn you, Daphne!' Leydecker said intensely. 'And damn your mother! That money was as much mine as it was hers!'

'But it was left to me,' Daphne said.

Leydecker, baffled and frustrated, left them. Julius looked at Daphne with puzzled eyes.

'Darling,' she said softly, 'you'd better go home now. We'll have a very busy day tomorrow.'

'Busy?' Julius asked, dazed.

'Of course. A wedding gown, dress clothes for you, a church for the wedding and some place for the wedding reception, and invitations, the photographers. Oh, a dozen things.'

'My mother won't go to a church,' Julius said in a small voice.

'Then we'll have a civil ceremony – although I did want to wear a wedding gown. Could we have the wedding in a temple?'

'My mother would go there,' Julius said, staggered, looking at Daphne for the first time, not quite seeing her.

'Then that's what we'll have to do,' Daphne said. 'We'll make those arrangements tomorrow.' She pecked him dryly on the cheek and hurried away.

Julius arrived home peculiarly numb, unable to think, his eyes blank.

'You're home early,' Mrs. Schapiro said with a drop of acid in each word.

Julius stared into the limbo that existed beyond the walls of the apartment, speechless.

'I'm surprised Miss Leydecker didn't keep you so late,' she said. 'Perhaps you had a little quarrel?'

Julius shook his head.

'No quarrel? Oh, my, how well you two must get along! Like two turtles! You never got along so well with your own momma, I'll bet, did you?'

Julius looked at his mother for a long moment.

'What's the matter? Cat got your tongue, my son?' Mrs Schapiro asked with elaborate sarcasm.

'I'm getting married,' Julius said in a small voice.

Mrs Schapiro was rocked into silence. Her mouth fell open. She opened it once and then again twice and yet nothing came out. She closed her eyes and breathed deeply. If her heart was going to go, now was the time. This was the hour. She watched for the failure of the vital organ. It did not stop. It laboured against the fat on her ribs but did not stop. A medical miracle. She would have to tell her doctor. Her son shot a bullet into her heart and it didn't stop. Worse than a bullet. A bomb. 'Well,' she finally exhaled, 'I'm glad you told me before the wedding. Some sons don't tell their mommas until afterwards – when it's all over. That's because they don't want their mommas to drop dead before the wedding. I see with you it don't matter. Either way it's all right. Eh, Julius?'

'I didn't know myself until tonight,' Julius said.

'Came as a surprise,' Mrs Schapiro said bitterly. 'All of a sudden an eagle flew down with a message: Julius Schapiro, get married. That's just what you need. Is that what happened, my son?'

'We're going to arrange for the temple tomorrow.' Julius said, still dazed, still unfeeling.

'A temple yet! It's going to be a regular wedding? Not some hotz-potz with a lawyer and the clerk from the City Hall?' Imagine the gall of the *shickseh*! right into a temple in front of the congregation, the rabbi, the Torah. She'd crawl down Moses's beard to get her son. A woman after a man was something terrible to see. To make Heaven ashamed. What gall!

'She wants to wear a wedding gown,' Julius explained weakly.

A shroud she should wear. A long white shroud. 'And this big society wedding with the *shickseh*, it's going to take place soon?'

147

'Pretty soon, I guess. Her father wants to go to California.'

'Oh, California – where all the movie stars live, eh? And he's taking you with him, my son?'

'No,' Julius said, shaking his head. 'Just him. He's going.'

'And her mother? She's staying here, of course?' Mrs Schapiro asked, her hands on her dumpy hips.

'I don't know. Maybe not. I've never met her mother,' Julius said.

'Well, that's all right,' Mrs Schapiro said with elaborate sarcasm. 'Even-Steven. I didn't meet your wife-to-be.'

'She'll be here tomorrow night,' Julius said.

'Maybe so, my son,' Mrs Schapiro said, 'maybe so. But the question is: Will *I* be here tomorrow night?'

Julius looked at his mother. 'Why? Where are you going, Ma?'

'Maybe to Heaven,' Mrs Schapiro said breathily. 'To join your blessed father. Maybe if they'll let me in. But maybe' – Mrs Schapiro started to breathe deeply, quickly, dangerously – 'they'll say to me when I get there: Sorry Mrs Schapiro but we don't let the mothers of fools and blockheads into this place. They won't want me! Why? Because I am a fool! I bled my life away in little pieces to raise one son – one little boy, and now that he's half grown to a man's size he picks up with a janitor's daughter and gets married! Is that what I slaved and bled for? Is that what your poppa, may he rest in peace, died for? No! No! No!' She shook her finger vigorously in Julius's face. 'If you bring that *shickseh* into this house, it'll be to see your dead mother! Do you hear?! Your dead mother! I'll be dead! Dead! Dead! You'll bury me in the Elmont cemetery before the wedding! I promise, Julius! I promise! Dead! Dead! Gone from this world! From this world! The worms will be eating me when you are on your honeymoon!' She fell to the floor on her knees. The sound startled Julius, who rose involuntarily from his chair. Mrs Schapiro rocked back and forth on her knees. 'God! God strike now! Now, now, stop the heart! Stop the heart!' She struck her breast an alarmingly hard blow. 'Let it stop! Stop! Let it stop!' She pulled her hair and began to shriek and wail and rocked. 'God! God! What have I done? What have I done? Dead! Dead! Dead! Stop it now! I beg you God! Stop the heart now! Let it stop! Let it stop!' She rocked wildly back and forth, wailing, clenching her hands, the perspiration mingled with her tears as her hair flew wildly from her face. 'What did I do to deserve this?! What did I do!' She let out an inhuman keening sound. 'Ooooooeeee! Oooooooahhhh! Ooooooaiiiii!'

'Ma, Ma,' Julius said, terrified, shaken, 'stop, stop.'

'I want to die! I want to die! To die! To die! Let me die!!'

Julius began to wrestle with his mother. 'Ma please, please, get up, get up.'

She flung him away from her. 'Let me die! Let me die! God – this minute – let me die!'

There was a commotion in the hall of the apartment. The doorbell rang.

'Ma, ma, the neighbours,' Julius said in an agony of embarrassment.

'Let them see! Let them hear!' Mrs Schapiro cried out, weepingly, hysterically. She lurched to her feet drunkenly and ran towards the door. She flung it open. 'Oh, oh, oh, I want to die!' Mrs Schapiro cried as she threw herself into the small knot of men and women at the door. They caught her, and she began to flounder, screaming, 'God, let me die! Let me die! I want to die!'

'It must be a gall-bladder attack,' someone said helpfully. 'The pain is terrific.'

'Mrs Schapiro! Mrs Schapiro!' the women cried out, anxious, frightened.

'Someone should call a doctor!' another helpful voice said.

'Is it the gall bladder, Mrs Schapiro?'

'Ooooooeee! I want to die! I don't want to live!'

'Where does it hurt, Mrs Schapiro?'

'Someone should call a doctor – the woman is in agony!'

'It's the heart? Does it hurt there, Mrs Schapiro?'

'So don't stand around like schlemiels, help her!'

'Who can help her when you don't know what's wrong?'

'I want to die! To die!'

'She's fainting! God in Heaven, get her some smelling salts!'

'It could be appendicitis?'

'Diabetes it's not. With that you go quiet!'

'Mrs Schapiro! Mrs Schapiro! What is it? What is it?'

'I don't want to live! I want to die!'

'Help me, she's heavy!'

'Julius! Julius! Why are you standing there like such a fool? Can't you see your mother needs help?'

'You mean – her son is there?'

'Come on, help me. We'll take her to my apartment!'

'What kind of sense is that? She's already in her apartment!'

'Don't argue, the woman is dying!'

'Take her into her own apartment!'

'Call a doctor, at least.'

'Mrs Schapiro, what hurts? What hurts? Tell us. So we can tell the doctor!'

'The *shickseh*! The *shickseh*!'

'Ahhh,' someone said.

'Is that all?'

'What do you mean is that all? That's plenty.'

'From *shicksehs* no one dies. Give her a glass of tea and lemon. She'll feel better.'

'Julius, you should be ashamed of yourself. Look what you're doing to your momma. And for a *shickseh*! Feh!'

'This is America. Let him marry who he pleases. I don't go for that Old Country stuff.'

'Another country heard from. Shut up, Mr Know-It-All-and-Can't-Hold-a-Job!'

'In my family, three sons married *shicksehs*. All three. Can you imagine that mother?'

'Don't talk about your family. Some family. I know those three. They were lucky they got *shicksehs*. Three bums!'

'Very fine college-educated young men, madam! I'll have you know!'

'A college from bums!'

'Come, Mrs Schapiro, come to my apartment!'

'Julius?! We're taking your mother to Mrs Herzberg's.'

The small knot of people disappeared from the door, and their talking with them. Julius got up and closed the door and went to his room. He sat on the edge of his bed in the darkness and stared out of the window, sightlessly, and wondered how he would like married life.

Evelyn liked Daphne when she met her. So did Mr Pollack. The news of Julius's marriage delighted them both, and Pollack hinted of a startling wedding present.

For Mrs Schapiro the unthinkable was taking place, and because she was curious she met Daphne, who was enchanting and thoughtful and considerate and listened when Mrs Schapiro chose to talk and listened when Julius chose to talk and spoke only when she was expected to speak. Before long the unthinkable was not so unthinkable. Bizarre, perhaps. But then the bizarre had its piquant aspects.

'Refined,' Mrs Schapiro told her neighbours. 'A refined girl. Not common. Not coarse. Refined. And very well travelled. Highly educated, in fact.'

Within a week Daphne and Mrs Schapiro were thick and conspiratorial, and Julius found that he was not needed.

A week later Mrs Schapiro delivered herself of this opinion: 'Better a refined Gentile girl than some common Jewish *yenteh*.' And so the unthinkable, which had become the bizarre, now became something else. By the day before the wedding Mrs Schapiro could not stop singing Daphne's praises. Her neighbours were delighted, superficially. Privately, in the sanctums of the kitchens, the opinions, by the women at any rate, were: 'Let her schmear her from head to toe. A *shickseh* she is.'

'But a pretty one,' the men maliciously reminded their wives.

'If *shicksehs* weren't pretty, who would marry them?' the women replied scornfully, resolving the charms of Daphne Leydecker once and for all.

Julius, still stunned by his mother's change of attitude, still bewildered by the marriage which seemed now to be rushing at him with express-train speed, confided in Evelyn. Evelyn listened patiently.

'What is it, Julius?' Evelyn finally asked.

'I don't know if I *want* to marry her,' Julius finally confessed.

'Don't you believe that she loves you?'

'But do I really love her? Or am I only infatuated with her?' Julius asked earnestly.

'Ask yourself that question twenty years from now,' Evelyn said soberly. 'Love is the big money. Infatuation is the small change. Everyone does with small change. The big money comes to just a few.'

'But her moral character,' Julius said unhappily.

'Julius,' Evelyn said, shifting her weight on the chair, 'I'm going to tell you a deep dark secret about women. The secret is this: all of them are liars. They never have as many boy friends as they claim, they never have as many virtues as they claim, they never have as many vices as they claim. They have more cunning than they are willing to admit and less intelligence than they pretend to. They are stronger than they let on and more cold-blooded than you'll ever find them. They kill themselves less often than men because they are less sensitive than men. They stay sane through much more than men can because they are less likely to be upset. Rapists are insane, and the men who cherish raped women go out of their minds with shame. Raped women don't lose much sleep. Why? Because God made man in a neurotic moment and woman in a practical afterthought. Life can go on without men. It would have to stop without women. And in important matters like that, God takes no chances with the weak, the unstable, and the unreliable. If you had gone through all that Daphne claims to have undergone, you would be a gibbering wreck. You can see she's no wreck.'

'Does that mean she lied to me about all those things?' Julius asked hopefully.

Evelyn looked at him. You talk to them and they don't understand you. 'Yes,' Evelyn said firmly, positively. 'I wouldn't be in the least surprised.'

'I had a sort of hunch that was so,' Julius said with a grin.

Be happy, sleep-walker. Smile and smile and walk in your dreams. To awake is dangerous. It might destroy you. 'Now you know a woman's secrets,' Evelyn said, 'be smart and don't let her know that you know.'

'Don't worry about me,' Julius said with a grin. 'I'll know how to handle her.'

Evelyn smiled. Well, that's my wedding present to you. Let's see Pollack top that.

Mrs Schapiro thought Mr Leydecker a handsome, well-set-up man. 'I hear you are planning to go to California, Mr. Leydecker?'

'That's right. This week, Mrs Schapiro.'

'On business, maybe?'

'Well, I'm going to live there – yes.'

'My, they say California is a wonderful place.'

'All places seem wonderful when you are starting out for them, Mrs Schapiro.'

'How true, how true, Mr Leydecker. They make a handsome couple, don't they?'

'Handsome, handsome.'

'I didn't know you were a widower. Julius thought your wife was still alive. Daphne told me the truth. Ah, how your wife would have loved to have seen this wedding!'

'Yes, indeed.'

'And Julius's father. Ahhh. It seems as though parents have but one thing to live for: to see their children happily married. How unfair your wife and my husband couldn't live to see that. Especially of only children.'

'Greatly unfair, Mrs Schapiro.'

'It will be so lonely without Julius in the house. I won't know what to do with myself.'

'Why? You are still a healthy vigorous woman. You could make yourself active and useful.'

'You really think so?'

'Of course! I think women ought to be self-sufficient. They ought to have their own lives!'

'Yes, but the loneliness, Mr Leydecker. The loneliness. Ah, that's something when you get on in years. You'll be lonely, too, out there in California – no friends, no daughter.'

'I suppose I will be.'

'Daphne used to cook and clean, I'll bet.'

'Yes, she did.'

'And took care of you when you were sick?'

'I'm rarely sick.'

Yes, but you're getting on. Not that you're not a wonderful-looking man, healthy and in the pink of condition. But, none of us is getting any younger, are we?'

'I suppose not.'

'Have you ever thought of – well, for companionship – marrying again?'

'Welll –'

'You ought to think of it seriously. I know that some people think it's not showing proper respect for the dead –'

'That's nonsense!'

'You think so?'

'Absolute rot! What's a woman to do when her husband dies? Throw herself on his grave? That's the barbarism of the Hindu suttee.'

'What's that?'

'Well, the custom in India was for women to throw themselves on the funeral pyre when their dead husbands were burned.'

'My, what a well-travelled man you are! Then you believe in remarriage – after – tragedy?'

'I most certainly do. You ought to have a husband.'

'For widows it's all right – but for widowers?'

'Well, of course it's right.'

'Then you are planning to marry again? What a lucky woman! Who is she, if I may ask?'

'Well, no one just yet.'

'Oh, my, what a catch some woman is missing!'

'Well, thank you, Mrs Schapiro.'

'You know, so long as we're sort of related – why don't we be less formal? Call me Sarah. And I'll call you –?'

'Ernest.'

'What a lovely name! Ernest. It just goes on the lips like – well, I don't know.'

'I don't like being called Ernie.'

'Who would? Some people have no taste. Ernest is the right name and the right way to say it. Would you believe it that some people call me Sadie?'

'Shocking. Sarah is a lovely name.'

Do you think so? Do you really think so?'

Hanrahan stepped up to the buffet table with Evelyn. He took some punch for himself and for Evelyn.

'I thought the ceremony quite interesting.'

'It has its charm,' Evelyn remarked as she took the punch.

'Frankly though, I have very little use for organized religion of any kind.'

'So the best people say,' Evelyn replied, sipping her punch.

'If I was to get married – I wouldn't want a religious ceremony of any kind.'

'Frankly, I'd settle for any kind – even a Shinto ceremony. I'm beyond being particular.'

'Now why do you say those things, Evelyn? You know you don't mean them.'

'You know that I know that I don't mean them?'

'Well, of course. There's a great capacity in you for religiosity.'

'Maybe. But as I said, it doesn't matter which religion. If you think Catholicism is so hotsy-totsy, then let it be Catholicism. For my taste it's six of one and three for a nickel of the other.'

'You're not a cynic. I don't believe that pose.'

'I am a cynic. All women are cynics.'

'Ah, female chauvinism.'

'I don't believe it.'

'You're a Truth Seeker, aren't you?'

'Strictly between us, I wanted to find a graceful way of disbanding the group and Leydecker agreed that a little white lie would turn the trick. I sympathize with them. But I see too clearly to be a Truth Seeker.'

'So do I, Francis. So do I.'

'What does that mean, Evelyn?'

'Francis – all women want men. With some it's a consuming lifelong passion. With others it's a passing fancy. And with others it's a hopeless drag. I don't mean just men to sleep with. I mean men to love and to comfort

157.

and to protect and to cherish. Women just don't want husbands. They want men. And half of them settle for their sons as cheerfully as one-quarter settle for their fathers and the final quarter settle for their husbands and lovers. I'm no different from the rest of my sex. I have no brother, and my father is a totally uninteresting man firmly in the grip of my mother and I have no son. I want a husband. I want a husband so badly that I am willing to get married anywhere, anytime, under any religion. Do it in Latin, do it in Hebrew, do it in Episcopalian English, do it in Low Dutch. But let those blessed words be said over me.'

'Ah, you're having fun at my expense.'

'Francis, when I talk about this don't let how I say what I say bemuse you into thinking that I don't mean every little word. Daphne got Julius. I can imagine how. In spite of Mrs Schapiro's dramatic performance heard over the whole lower East Bronx and parts of Manhattan. That's because Daphne wanted Julius. I want you Francis. But I can't do it the same way Daphne did. She's got the advantages of weight, age, and craft over me. Francis – you're a sleep-walker – as bad as Julius – but in a different way. The first day I met you I should have walked you out of Pollack's office down to City Hall and blitzed you. My fault was that I lingered. Lingering leads to death, as they always say.'

'But, Evelyn, we will get married.'

'In some other world. Not here. You discovered religiosity in me to make me think that being a Jew I couldn't be happy with a Hanrahan. Francis, I am beyond being a Jew. I'm beyond everything. I'm a forty-four-year-old corset problem. There's honesty for you. And what does it raise in you?'

'Respect.'

'Forgive me, but I spit on your respect.'

'Ah, you're being bitter.'

'Being honest. They are synonyms, Francis.'

'My mother is an old woman. Evelyn – when she passes away –'

'If I honestly thought her death would ring out the wedding bells, I'd push her off the Staten Island ferry. But it won't. You'd ask me to wait for a decent interval. Just to respect the dead. I won't wait. Not through the rest of her life or through the mourning. Francis, we're through.'

'Evelyn, be fair!'

'All's fair in love and war, Francis!'

'We're not children –'

'Precisely why I can't wait. I've waited too long. I won't wait another day.'

'What would you want me to do?'

'Leave this place with me right now and go down to the Municipal Building and get a licence. I'll pack a small bag and we'll go away for the weekend and when we come back on Monday the waiting period will be over and we can be married.'

'Live with you in sin over the weekend?'

'And we'll have a hell of a good time, Francis. I'm fat but I'm active and I haven't got a prudish bone in my body.'

'Ah, Evelyn! You're joking me, aren't you? Is that a way for us to begin our lives together?'

'Hanrahan – go to hell,' Evelyn said, and put down her punch glass and walked away. Hanrahan started after her and then stopped. He rubbed his chin unhappily and went back to the punch bowl.

Their plane droned over the Atlantic to Bermuda, and Julius linked his fingers with Daphne's. She turned from the window to give him a radiant smile.

'Penny for your thoughts, Mrs Schapiro,' Julius said, lowering his voice.

She put her head next to his. 'Julius,' she said dreamily.

'Yes, darling?'

I've been thinking about what you're going to do afterwards.'

'Now, Daphne,' Julius said coyly.

'I meant after the honeymoon,' Daphne replied with a giggle.

'What do you mean?' Julius asked.

'Well, working for Mr Pollack was all right when you were single. But now that you're married – well, it doesn't seem like the right sort of a job for you.'

'What ought I to do?'

'Well, you know Gus, don't you?'

'Gus?'

'August? The young fellow with a beard?'

Oh, is that his name?'

'August Fleckenberg is his whole name. Well, Gus is a sort of writer and he does television shows and he knows lots of people in television and in advertising and I thought he could find something for you. I know he'd try – for my sake.'

'Say, did you and Gus –' He hesitated, and jealousy rose in him remembering the evening the young man with the beard offered to prove the fact of love in public.

'Of course not, silly,' Daphne said with a teasing smile.

'Course not what?' Julius demanded.

'Course not whatever you thought Gus and I ever did.'

Julius was about to speak but Daphne bit his ear lobe. He tingled with pleasure. 'Well,' he said after a while, 'maybe you're right about TV. I'll talk to Al and Lou when I come back. They may have an idea.'

'Oh, never mind them,' she said sweetly. 'I'll get you something – somehow.'

They turned their eyes towards the fast-setting sun as their plane winged south.

'A nice Jewish kid,' Al said a bit drunkenly to Julius's second cousin, who came from Brooklyn. She wore a large corsage and her tightest dress and the new shade of pale lipstick.

'Oh, he's a doll,' she said, anxious lest any of the wedding party had noticed that they had slipped out for a drink. 'Of course our families haven't been too close. I mean, we live in Brooklyn.'

'Way the hell out there, hunh?' Al said admiringly.

'Oh, but I don't have to go home tonight,' she said. 'We're sleeping over at Aunt Sadie's place if we want to – although we don't have to.'

'The hell you are,' Al said. 'You know damned well where you're sleeping tonight, baby, don't you?'

The second cousin giggled. 'Really, Al, you say the most awful things. A person who just met you might think God knows what!'

'That's right, honey,' Al said with a smile. 'I'm harmless.'

'Harmless all right. I'll say. About as harmless as an atom bomb.'

'Without the fallout,' Al said, and winked.

The second cousin stifled a whoop. 'You're terrrrible!'

'You're a nice Jewish kid,' Al said, sidling closer. 'You don't think I'd hurt a nice Jewish kid, would you? Like my own sister. My own sister.' He patted her tenderly.

'You wouldn't do that to your own sister!'

Al laughed richly and hit the table with his enormous hand. 'Funneeeee! Funneee!'

'Is it true that Julius is going into TV?'

'Hell, yes! Maybe not with our current project. But we like the kid. We're going to find something for him! Mark my words. When Al Douglas makes a promise – sister – I keep it!'

'It must be awfully glamorous being in TV. Have I seen any of your shows?'

'Baby – you haven't seen the best of them – yet.'

The second cousin smiled and wriggled a little but not too hard. After all, she wanted a man, too. 'Some sister I'm turning out to be.'

This is the philosopher's hour, someone thought. The litter of the wedding party was becoming soggy, the coffee stains hardening in the cups. The final drunks sleeping fitfully. The women long since gone. But Pollack spoke on, and Julius's uncles, two of whom were still sober, listened along with Leydecker, who was stonily drunk, staying upright out of some dim racial memory of the position, his eyes fixed unblinkingly on a thought which had long ago solidified and had become motionless.

Pollack talked. 'I see, in our world, very little room for the man of culture. For the man who cares for the spiritual values, the humanistic man.'

The employees of the caterers stored away the dishes in heavy cartons, and a disheartened Negro listlessly pushed a broom.

Pollack talked.

On Staten Island, Hanrahan let himself into his home and noted that the television set was off. He steadied himself against the frame of the door. Punch, finally, had become too weak for his tastes after Evelyn left.

Above all, he did not want to awaken his mother.

Evelyn's mother came into her bedroom.

'You're home early, dear. Was it a nice wedding?'

'The best,' Evelyn said. 'The combined ages of the bride and groom are a sum less than my own. I thought of that just now.'

'If going to weddings depresses you so much, you shouldn't go,' her mother observed.

'Weddings don't depress me. They comfort me,' Evelyn said.

'Would you like some tea?'

'I'd like a drink. But not tea. Would you bring me a little rye?'

'Didn't you drink at the wedding?'

'No. I talked. Isn't that what's wrong with me, Mom? I talk instead of drinking?'

Her mother looked at her disapprovingly and left. She came back shortly with a shot glass. Evelyn took the drink and held it up. '*L'chaim!*' she said and downed the drink and turned the shot glass in her hand for a moment. 'Mom, what does "*L'chaim*" mean? Good health?'

'No,' her mother said, 'it means – to life.'

Evelyn nodded her understanding.

'Go to sleep, dear,' her mother said. 'You'll feel better in the morning.'

Evelyn smiled. Trust her mother to come up with the truth about *Weltschmerz*.

Mrs Schapiro brushed her long hair in front of her mirror. In Julius's bed two of his cousins were asleep, their faces creamed, their hairdos carefully protected with bandannas. One of them was a snorer. Another cousin was unaccounted for. Mrs Schapiro assumed that she had gone home to Brooklyn. She looked at herself in the mirror. What would she do once the nieces went home? There was just so much she could expect from her neighbours and just so much she could expect from her relatives. She would have to do for herself. Leydecker had given her his address in Los Angeles and said he would be glad to escort her when she arrived. The trick was to catch him before he met too many people in Los Angeles, particularly hungry widows. The idea of remarrying was definitely in his mind. Carefully planted there. Was she going to let some other woman enjoy the fruit when the plant came up? She'd be out there a week after he was. That was her decision. She was saving her husband's insurance for her old age. But this was an investment. Not like spending. Investing. In the future. Like United States savings bonds. So he wasn't Jewish. So what? What did she want? An old Jewish buck with his children and his relatives and his friends and his dead wife's relatives and friends? Leydecker was alone. That much was apparent. For Leydecker she could be the whole world and what more could any woman ask? What he needed was a good Jewish wife. That would make something of him. If he was a cabinet-maker, then he was a skilled worker. And if he was a skilled worker, they'd always have enough. Mrs Ernest Leydecker. What a name! And yet what's a name? And a nice-looking man, too. Refined. Well-travelled. Strong-looking, too. Mrs Schapiro suddenly giggled and looked guiltily over her shoulder into the next room. The nieces slept on, the snorer undisturbed.

Pollack talked while the table was cleared from in front of him. Leydecker was jarred and swayed danger-ously in his chair. One of Julius's uncles caught Leydecker and thought that the father of the bride ought to be taken home. Another uncle said he would take them in his car but he was too fascinated by Pollack to stop listening. The lights in the catering hall began to flicker. A hint? A warning? The uncles rose, hauling the heavy Leydecker to his feet. And Pollack talked as he walked along with them. Art, science, humanity, religion, the theatre, morals, folkways and mores, yesterday, today, and tomorrow. And so they made their way to the late spring street. The warm moist promise of summer in the air. Leydecker was heavily loaded into the rear of the car with one uncle and Pollack stationed himself in the front seat. The other uncle got behind the wheel of the car and started the motor. The car pulled away from the kerb into the night and Pollack still talked.

In the darkness of Al's bedroom the second cousin writhed.

'Oh, Al, Al, do you love me?'

'Like for ever baby,' Al said hoarsely.

And the sleep-walkers covered each other's mouths with undying love.

Summer, which falls on New York like a fetid blanket, hung still in the sky, waiting to drop. Any moment. Now it was possible for the air to be soft and lulling. Pollack, who had cast off his winter garments, now came to the office in a seersucker suit. His plans for the summer were made, the contracts signed, the phone rang constantly. The Comédie-Française would not be available next season and so the opportunity was lost to Pollack. Julius, who had returned from his honeymoon, had not returned to Theodore Pollack Productions. He had, instead, gone to Los Angeles with Daphne and was now working in television. Leydecker had gone to Los Angeles and so had Mrs. Schapiro, and the last postcard Evelyn had received from Julius bore the announcement of his mother's engagement to Leydecker. Al Douglas and Lou Cohen had gone to Los Angeles, and Evelyn had heard that one of Julius's female cousins had gone to Los Angeles. Hanrahan had asked for a transfer to Los Angeles.

'The end of the world is coming,' Evelyn remarked. 'Everyone is going to Los Angeles. All the sleep-walkers, all the lotus eaters, all the cocaine sniffers are going to Los Angeles. New York will be left to the realistic cats and me. This may turn into a sensible town after all.'

'I shall never abandon New York,' Pollack declared. 'This is where my true world lies. This is my heartland.'

'Yes, but you can't live for ever,' Evelyn said. 'And you are the last sleep-walker.'

Pollack refused to argue with Evelyn. 'It's a pity Julius chose to give up the legitimate stage. You know, I was going to make him a full partner. That was to be my wedding present.'

Evelyn shook her head. 'What a present. Come eat the lotus with me – you have a full share.'

'I sometimes think, Evelyn,' Pollack said frostily, 'that you are not equipped to understand the theatre. It is not merely a business. It is a vocation. Like the church, or the arts of war.'

Evelyn gave up. It was no use. But she was lonely in the office when Pollack was gone and she missed seeing Julius at the desk across the room. There had been no one there for months. She was about to speak to Pollack concerning the matter when he told her that they were to have a new reader.

'Not a girl, please,' Evelyn said.

'No, a young man. In fact, a relative of Julius's. I met his father at Julius's wedding and we had a long talk. He told me about his son's ambitions to be in the theatre. The legitimate theatre.'

'Well, imagine that,' Evelyn said fliply, but was pleased, for once, by Pollack's sense of order, of tidiness. 'And what is his name?'

'David. David Eisenstadt,' Pollack said. 'I shall be away the week he starts. But I'm sure you can tell him what his duties are. He will, of course, start at a much lower figure. What was Julius getting?'

'Forty-five dollars a week.'

'I think David ought to start at thirty,' Pollack said. 'Let him work up.'

'Let him live,' Evelyn said softly. 'Give him forty.'

'His father is quite well to do,' Pollack remarked. 'He doesn't need the money. It is to be close to the theatre.'

'In that case why pay him anything?' Evelyn asked.

'Don't be ridiculous,' Pollack remarked. 'I shall be back after the Fourth of July weekend for a day or so. I'm sure things can be left in your hands.'

'I'm sure,' Evelyn said dryly with a smile. And then Pollack was gone. Gone to the mountains. Gone to his audience. Gone to his art in hotels. Gone to be the producer. To eat the lotus.

One Monday morning Evelyn approached the door in the long darkened hallway that led to the office and saw a young man in a neat summer suit, with thick glasses loitering nearby. It was David Eisenstadt, Evelyn thought. There was no doubt about it. She went to the door and took out her key. The young man hung back slightly, uncertain. She opened the door and pushed it back and stepped down on the doorstop. 'Come on in, David,' she called over her shoulder.

He entered the office, and as she combed her hair in the mirror near Pollack's door she could watch him. He entered the office as one enters a place of worship, slowly, reverently, raptly, frightened and touched and expectant. She stripped out the combings from her comb and dropped the ball into a wastebasket.

'That's your desk,' she said, pointing.

He moved to the desk and touched it with tentative fingers, looking at the stack of manuscripts, at the dusty coffee jar filled with pencils.

'Go ahead and sit down. The chair isn't holy,' Evelyn said.

David smiled gratefully and showed small, childlike white teeth. He sat down behind the desk and then turned in the swivel chair.

'My name is Evelyn,' she said.

He nodded his head.

'Pollack is away,' Evelyn said. 'He'll be back sometime the middle of next week. Until he comes back you can use the john in his office.' Evelyn sat down and looked at him. 'And what do you want to become in the American theatre?'

David looked at her through his thick glasses uncomprehendingly.

'What's the matter, no spika da englis?'

'No,' David said in a thin voice. 'I mean, yes, I do, of course.

'What do you want to become in the theatre? Writer? Actor? Director? Producer? House manager? Ticket chopper? What?'

David considered for a moment. 'I want to become something,' he said. 'I'm not sure. But I want to become something – someone important.' His voice got deeper and his face took on a far-off look of exaltation. It was a look Evelyn knew very well.

'Yes,' Evelyn said. 'I know just what you mean. You're another sleep-walker. Like the rest. Well, go ahead. I won't wake you up.' Even as she said it bitterly she knew that she was lying. One day she would try. It would be an intolerable world if she did not try.

MORE ABOUT PENGUINS

If you have enjoyed reading this book you may
wish to know that *Penguin Book News* appears every
month. It is an attractively illustrated magazine containing
a complete list of books published by Penguins and
still in print, together with details of the month's
new books. A specimen copy will be sent free on
request.

Penguin Book News is obtainable from most bookshops;
but you may prefer to become a regular subscriber at
3s for twelve issues. Just write to Dept EP, Penguin
Books Ltd, Harmondsworth, Middlesex, enclosing
a cheque or postal order, and you will be put on the
mailing list.

Some other books published by Penguins are described on
the following pages.

Note: *Penguin Book News* is not available in the U.S.A.

JOURNEY TO THE END OF THE NIGHT

Louis-Ferdinand Céline

Louis-Ferdinand Céline was one of the major European writers of the thirties. Only the fact that he collaborated with the Vichy government in France during World War II, and his consequent public denigration by free French governments, have made him a post-war 'forgotten man'.

His works are epics of adamant pessimism, of the belief – common to writers living in the between-the-wars shadow – that man is fundamentally ignoble.

Journey to the End of the Night is the first of two autobiographical novels. It is the story of Ferdinand Bardamu, and his search for personal fulfilment in war, the lower depths of Paris, through African jungles, and finally in the slums of the United States and the factories of Detroit. It is a violent, exciting odyssey, told with distinctive vividness and sensitivity.

'It is not reality which Céline paints but the hallucinations which reality provokes. I find here the accents of a remarkable sensibility' – André Gide

In the Penguin Modern Classics

Not for sale in the U.S.A. or Canada

OWLS AND SATYRS

David Pryce-Jones

Is the best education that money can buy
any defence against life's realities?

What follows when a young man comes on his mother's
lover surreptitiously leaving the family home in the early
hours?
Helen, the worldly sister, might accept the position.
But Henry was discontented, rebellious, confused. How
would he react if his widowed mother chose to marry
again?

Against the fashionable background of 'Eton, Oxford and
the Guards' a new writer works out the uncomfortable
answers to a problem common to all humanity. His novel
is 'as swift and succinct as a story by Françoise Sagan' –
Observer

Not for sale in the U.S.A.

THE GROUP
Mary McCarthy

The runaway best-selling story of eight eager, innocent girl graduates starting life in 1933 – pioneering their way from sex and interior décor to cooking and contraception . . .

'Outrageous, outspoken, outsmarting and outstripping all other fiction on the course for high-octane performance' – Kenneth Allsop

The impact of *The Group* has been tremendous – measurable in the 300,000 copies already sold before Penguin publication. It has now been released as a United Artists film, directed by Sidney Lumet.

'Extremely funny and totally adult' – *Sunday Times*

Also by David Karp

LEAVE ME ALONE

David Karp's previous novels have been compared with
Orwell's *Nineteen Eighty-Four*, Koestler's *Darkness at
Noon*, and Huxley's *Brave New World*. *Leave Me Alone* is
a savage satire on the morals and manners of
contemporary American suburbanites. It concerns Arthur,
a junior editor in a distinguished New York publishing
house, and Eleanor, his wife. For the sake of their two
children they leave their New York apartment and buy a
house in commuter country. Against that background –
with Arthur a fiery individualist and Eleanor a rigid
conformist – conflict is inevitable.

Leave Me Alone is a frightening book by a novelist of
indignation and a passionate critic of social inadequacies.

Not for sale in the U.S.A. or Canada.